"I can't sleep without a pillow."

"Oh, for—" Brian glared at her, then pulled her to him so that her head rested in the hollow of his shoulder. "Will this help?"

Juliana nodded against his chest. "Thank you," she said unsteadily.

Brian didn't answer. He didn't move. He tried to ignore the warmth of her body, her faint womanly scent, the pressure of her breasts against his side.

Juliana murmured sleepily and burrowed closer. He swore under his breath, and she put her arm across his chest, burning her brand across his skin. It was too much. It was past bearing.

With a low groan, he grasped her chin and turned her face to his. Her eyes flew open. An exclamation rose from her lips, but Brian stopped it with his mouth. He felt her surprised resistance, but he didn't stop. He couldn't stop.

Dear Reader,

When two people fall in love, the world is suddenly new and exciting, and it's that same excitement we bring to you in Silhouette Intimate Moments. These are stories with scope, with grandeur. The characters lead the lives we all dream of, and everything they do reflects the wonder of being in love.

Longer and more sensuous than most romances, Silhouette Intimate Moments novels take you away from everyday life and let you share the magic of love. Adventure, glamour, drama, even suspense— these are the passwords that let you into a world where love has a power beyond the ordinary, where the best authors in the field today create stories of love and commitment that will stay with you always.

In coming months look for novels by your favorite authors: Maura Seger, Parris Afton Bonds, Linda Howard, and Nora Roberts, to name just a few. And whenever you buy books, look for all the Silhouette Intimate Moments, love stories *for* today's women *by* today's women.

Leslie J. Wainger
Senior Editor
Silhouette Books

Barbara Faith

Asking for Trouble

Dear Carolyn:
Best wishes,
Barbara

Silhouette Intimate Moments

Published by Silhouette Books New York

America's Publisher of Contemporary Romance

SILHOUETTE BOOKS
300 East 42nd St., New York, N.Y. 10017

ISBN: 0-373-07208-2

First Silhouette Books printing September 1987

BARBARA FAITH

is very happily married to an ex-matador whom she met when she lived in Mexico. After a honeymoon spent climbing pyramids in the Yucatan, they settled down in California—but they're vagabonds at heart. They travel at every opportunity, but Barbara always finds the time to write.

Chapter 1

She was nondescript, just another woman in the Pan Am line, a typical tourist dressed in flat shoes and a polyester print dress a size too large. A straw hat with a red, white and blue band proclaiming I Love Miami Beach partially hid her mud-brown hair.

The monitor on the wall above the ticket agent updated its information. Flight 247 to Rio de Janeiro would be forty-five minutes late leaving Miami.

Perspiration broke out on the woman's upper lip.

After the passengers were checked in they made their way to the gate. In the crowded waiting room she sat alone and tried to read a book about the beautiful sights of Rio—Copacabana Beach, Sugar Loaf Mountain, Guanabara Bay. But Juliana Thornton knew she wouldn't see any of them. Two hours after she landed in Rio she'd change planes for Belém.

From Belém she would take a ferry to the small island country of San Benito.

The forty-five minutes crept by with agonizing slowness. When at last the flight was called Juliana followed the other passengers to the boarding platform. She handed her ticket to the flight attendant and pretended to look into the plastic bag she carried while the other woman glanced at it. When it was handed back Juliana mumbled her thanks and quickly boarded the plane. She then took her seat by the window and fastened her seat belt. She didn't look up when an elderly woman with blue hair took the seat beside her and said, "Well it's about time! I hate these delays, don't you?"

Juliana nodded, then looked quickly away. Her mouth was dry, and her heart was beating a staccato rhythm against her ribs. She closed her eyes, tipped the straw hat low over her face, and pretended to sleep.

After the rest of the passengers had found their seats the attendants did a last-minute check. Then they closed the big doors and the plane began to move. At last the muscles in Juliana's stomach began to relax. She'd made it! She'd gotten away from them.

The "them" were the federal authorities in Miami, more specifically an agent named Harry Bellows. From the moment he'd knocked on the door of her apartment overlooking Biscayne Bay, Juliana had felt uneasy. There was something about him that spelled bully. She could picture him at ten, as overweight and red-faced as he was today, tormenting every younger kid in the school yard.

"I want to talk to you about your brother's death," he'd said as he flashed his credentials.

She opened the door. As soon as he was inside he looked her up and down and without being asked to sit down, sprawled at one end of her lemon-colored sofa and loosened his black string tie. "Heard from that Latin lover of yours lately?"

There was an expression on his face, a loose-lipped look of such sly insinuation, that for a moment Juliana had felt a sickening sense of fear. Then her fear had been replaced by anger. She stood looking down at him, arms folded across her chest because that's where his eyes were riveted, and said, "I haven't seen or heard from Mr. Martinez in over a month."

"And you have no idea where he is. Wouldn't tell us if you did, would you?"

"Probably not." Juliana lifted her chin as she spoke and there was fire in her cinnamon eyes. It was the same fire that had glared defiantly back at the police when she'd taken part in a demonstration last year at the nuclear plant at Turkey Point.

"Think you're pretty cute, don't you, missy? Don't matter to you at all that Emilio Martinez and that bunch of revolutionaries he belongs to killed your brother." Bellows took out a soiled handkerchief and mopped his face. "It plain beats the hell out of me how you could turn your back on your own kin and not give a damn that it was your boyfriend who put a bullet in your own brother's head."

Juliana felt the color drain from her face and she held on to a chair back for support. Trying to speak calmly, she said, "I've told the police, and I've told the federal authorities that Mr. Martinez was with me the night Tim was killed. We had dinner together on Key Biscayne and then we went dancing. It was after midnight when he brought me back here. The police report said that Tim was killed around nine. Emilio couldn't possibly have been involved."

"Even if you're telling the truth, which I don't believe, don't think that lets your boyfriend off the hook because he sure as God was a part of it. Wouldn't be surprised if that foreigner Tim was married to wasn't part of it too. She's the one introduced you to Martinez, isn't she? You heard from her since she and her kid skipped the country?"

"Maria didn't skip the country, Mr. Bellows." Juliana clenched her hands together to keep from picking up the vase of daisies in the center of the coffee table and throwing it at him. "She was called back to San Benito because her father was ill."

She'd wondered at that time whether or not to tell him about Maria's phone call the previous night, about the fear in Maria's voice when she'd told her how bad things were in San Benito. Julie paused to recall the conversation. "I wish I had never left Miami," Maria had said.

"What's happened? Are you and Rafael all right?"

"Yes, for now. But..." Maria's voice had trembled and she'd started to cry. "I wish you were here. If I could just talk to you..."

Juliana had tightened her hand around the phone. "I'll come if you want me to."

"Would you, Julie? No...I don't know, I shouldn't ask..."

"You're family," Juliana had said. "You and Rafael. If you're in trouble I want to help. I'll come as soon as I can, Maria. I'll call you just before I leave Miami."

"No! Don't call me. Just go to the Hotel Carmen in San Benito and wait until I call you. And Julie, please don't tell anyone you're coming because..."

The line had gone dead.

Juliana had called the operator. The operator had tried to reconnect them, then reported that there seemed to be a malfunction on all the circuits to the island of San Benito.

Juliana had debated about telling Harry Bellows. She didn't like him but he had worked with her brother. Perhaps the agency could find out what was happening in San Benito. So she'd told him about the phone call and that she was concerned about Tim's wife and his five-year-old son.

But Bellows hadn't been concerned about either Maria or her son. "Hell, woman," he'd said, "don't fret yourself about her. She's probably another revolutionary just like Martinez and all those other Latinos." He stood and hitched up his pants. "There's lots more questions we got to ask you, Miss Thornton, and let me tell you, we aim to get some answers. I'm going to keep my eye on you, so don't you dare try to leave town."

Maybe it was the word *dare* that did it, Julie thought as the DC-10 sped down the runway. That and her

concern for Tim's widow and the little boy she loved
so much. As soon as Bellows left Julie had gone to the
phone. It had taken several hours and more than a
dozen phone calls before she found somebody who
knew somebody who would, for a price, give her a
fake passport. She went to the bank and withdrew
eight thousand dollars, almost depleting her bank ac-
count. The following day she went to a small import
shop just off Flagler Street. She gave the woman behind the counter her name and three thousand dollars. The woman closed the shop and drove Juliana to
a house in South Miami. There she was given the mud-
brown wig to cover her red hair and the polyester dress
to hide her figure. Makeup covered the sprinkle of
freckles across her cheeks and nose. Her naturally
thick brows were darkened by a heavy pencil, lines
were drawn around her eyes and nose, and her picture
was taken.

The name on the passport read Gertrude Weiser.
The age given was forty-four.

Juliana stayed at the house in South Miami until the
fake passport was ready and a flight to Brazil had been
arranged. She had brought a few clothes with her; she
would buy whatever else she needed at the airport in
Rio or in San Benito.

Juliana knew very little about San Benito. She'd
asked Tim about it once, knowing that's where he'd
met Maria. "Just another island," he'd said in his
pragmatic way. "Beaches and palm trees."

But that wasn't the way Maria had described it.
"San Benito is a paradise," Maria said. "The white

sand beaches are finer and cleaner than the sand on any of the other islands, and the water is so crystal clear you can see small fish swimming around your feet. The sun shines every day; the trade winds cool the nights. In the early morning a veil of mist covers the mountains so that you can barely see Manitura, the sleeping volcano."

To Juliana's question about whether or not Manitura had ever erupted, Maria said, "Only once, many years ago, before my great-grandparents came to San Benito from Spain. But that was long ago, now he only rumbles to let us know he's still there."

Maria's sea-green eyes softened as she continued. "At dawn each day the fishermen push their boats into the sea. Later, when it's light, you can see them casting their yellow butterfly nets into the water. San Benito is a magical island, Julie. I hope someday that I can show it to you."

A magical island. Juliana closed her eyes, to sleep and dream of a place where the beaches were clean and white and where the sun shone every day.

As the plane circled in for a landing, she could see the reflection of the lights of Rio shining on the curve of Copacabana Beach. It wouldn't be long now. Soon she would be in San Benito. She thought of Harry Bellows and of the agency's warning not to leave the country. When they discovered she wasn't in Miami, would they suspect that she had gone to San Benito? With a chill of fear she wondered if they would send anyone after her.

* * *

"I'll find her," Brian McNeely said. "I'll bring her back if I have to hog-tie her and sling her over my shoulder."

"I still can't believe she'd leave the country. I'd heard that she and Martinez split, so it surprised the hell out of me when we found out she'd taken off for San Benito." Jack Kelly drummed nervous fingers on his desk and frowned. "It's my fault, Brian. I shouldn't have sent Bellows out to see her. He's got about as much tact as a bulldozer and he's hated Latinos ever since the Cubans started coming to Miami in the sixties. It doesn't matter to him that they've added a lot to our community and that they've helped make Miami an international city. Bellows is a redneck with a one-track mind." Jack looked across his desk at Brian. "Have you ever met Julie Thornton?"

"Yes, about a year ago. I met her at a party. She was there with Tim and Maria." Brian leaned back in his chair. He still remembered the way Juliana looked that night, and how every other woman at the party, even a beauty like Maria Thornton, had paled by comparison.

She'd worn some kind of a blue-sequined T-shirt over a short black skirt, black stockings, high-heeled black shoes, and a blue-sequined tam over her curly red hair. She'd looked saucy and smart and incredibly desirable.

"She's a redhead," Brian told Jack. "Ten years younger than Tim. That would make her what... twenty-four or five? She's bright and she's commit-

ted—an activist—always out marching for a cause."
He grinned in spite of himself. "Tim had bailed her
out of jail for marching against something or other the
afternoon of the night I met her. He was so damned
mad that night he barely spoke to her."

Brian shifted his six-foot-three frame in the big
leather chair, remembering how he'd zeroed in on Juliana that night, and how she'd looked up at him with
those wide cinnamon eyes that were framed by long
dark lashes and full eyebrows. There'd been a slightly
mocking smile on her face when she'd said, "My God,
another cop. Tim's told me about you. He said you
were the best in the business, relentless and tough in
your pursuit of the bad guys." She'd laughed a throaty
laugh that made him want to pick her up and carry her
out of the room to some dark and quiet place, and
he'd vowed that before the night was over he'd kiss
that mocking smile right off her face.

He had kissed Juliana that night. When he took her
home after the party she tossed him a "Good night,
Elliot Ness!"—whereupon he caught her in his arms
and kissed her angrily and forcefully. After one small
gasp of surprise she began to kiss him back, respond-
ing with a passion that left his knees weak. When he
let her go her lips had been parted and her eyes had
looked smoky and dazed. Without a word she'd
turned and gone into her apartment.

Brian had called her every night for two weeks before she'd agreed to see him again. They went to a
place in Fort Lauderdale for dinner. She wore a pale

pink suit that made her look as appetizing as a strawberry soda.

They'd argued about U.S. military policies, Central American conflicts and nuclear waste. He thought she was the most beautiful woman he'd ever seen and wondered if she was too young for him—and whether or not he could keep his hands off her until they left the restaurant. After dinner he'd driven down to the beach and Julie had taken her shoes off and run down to the water's edge. He'd gone after her. It hadn't mattered that the water washed up over his loafers when he kissed her because it had been just as he remembered.

She'd resisted at first, then her lips had softened. Again Brian had felt his knees grow weak as an urgency of desire like nothing he had ever known before surged through his body. He held her away, looking down at her. She was too young for him, he didn't approve of her, they had nothing in common, but . . . She swayed toward him and he kissed her again and felt the warmth and softness of her body against his. He'd wanted to get lost in her, to hold her and never let her go.

She'd stepped away from him. There was an uncertainty, an expression of doubt in her dark eyes.

When Brian took her home he wanted to ask if he could go in with her, but she'd been silent on the way back. "I'll call you," he said. She'd nodded but hadn't looked at him.

He had called. He called every night for a month and her answer was always the same. "Sorry, I'm busy.'' Then he heard that she was dating Emilio Martinez and he felt like a damn fool. That had been over six months ago. He'd seen her at Tim's funeral, but they hadn't spoken.

"She works for a local television station," Jack Kelly said, breaking in on Brian's thoughts. "I contacted them but they haven't any idea where she is. Where do you think she's gone? San Benito?"

"I think she's wherever Martinez is," Brian said. "I'm going after her, Jack, and I'm going after her boyfriend." His voice hardened. "Tim Thornton was one of my best friends. I can't stand the thought of his sister running away to one of the men responsible for his murder."

Jack reached for a cigarette. "When are you leaving?"

"Tomorrow morning."

"Got any leads?"

"The sister-in-law. She was Maria Espinosa before she married. She went back to San Benito a month ago."

"Yeah, she'll probably know where Juliana is. I remember Tim saying his sister was crazy about the little boy." Jack got to his feet and stood facing Brian. "I think you're wrong about her. I know she's a rebel and that she and Tim didn't always agree, but I can't believe she'd have anything to do with Martinez if she honestly thought he was involved in Tim's murder." Jack waited and when Brian didn't answer he shrugged and said, "Stop downstairs before you leave. They'll have a check ready, and whatever else you need." He clapped Brian on the shoulder. "You take care of yourself. I'd tell you to give the local boys in San Benito a call if you need help, but I'm not sure how many of them can be trusted. The country's on the verge of a revolution, Brian. They've got guerrillas fighting in the mountains, and they've been smuggling arms into San Benito from Florida. That's what Tim was working on when he was killed. It's a dirty business. God only know how many people are involved. I'm afraid you'll be on your own there."

"Don't worry, I'll manage. I'll find Martinez and I'll find the Thornton woman."

I'll find her, Brian told himself, and when I do... He took a deep breath. The thought of Juliana Thornton hung in the air like a drift of smoke.

Chapter 2

Juliana awoke to music and the sound of voices. She lay for a few minutes staring up at the slowly moving overhead fan and knew she'd never felt so alone or so frustrated in her entire life.

For three days now she'd been waiting at the Hotel Carmen for Maria's call. She didn't know what to do or where to find Maria. She'd spent hour after hour in the uncomfortably warm room. She ate all her meals in the hotel, being careful to tell the desk clerk where she was and to ask him to call her if there were any telephone calls. She didn't know how much longer she could sit and do nothing.

Finally Juliana got up, slipped into the robe that lay at the foot of her bed, and went to stand at the window overlooking the street. Below there was a pandemonium of a revelry to rival Carnival in Rio. Crowds of people danced in the street behind a hometown band of trumpets and drums and fiddles. From the central plaza came the sound of bells and horns blowing.

"It's our annual wine festival," the clerk at the front desk told Juliana when she went downstairs. "It begins each year on the third day of September. It will last until midnight tomorrow. Tonight everyone will wear costumes and there will be dancing in the streets." He shook his finger at Juliana. "You mustn't stay in your room, *señorita*. You're a young and beautiful lady, you must go out tonight and join the celebration."

"Perhaps I will." Juliana forced a smile, knowing of course that she wouldn't.

That night when she went down to dinner wearing an emerald-green cotton dress, she discovered she was the only one in the dining room. She ordered a salad and when the waiter served it he put a glass of white wine beside her plate.

"Everyone must drink wine tonight," he said with a kindly smile. "When you have finished your dinner you should go out and join in the fun. If you don't wish to dance, then sit in a sidewalk café and watch the others. You might as well, you know, it will be impossible to sleep tonight."

It was after nine when Juliana stepped out of the hotel. She paused for a moment, listening to the noise and the laughter and the music. Girls in colorful costumes danced past her on the arms of handsome young men. An oompah band marched by. A man in a bear costume, with a garland of flowers around his neck, spotted her. Before she could protest he pulled her out of the doorway, whirled her around and around, then took one of the flowers from his garland, bowed, and handed it to her.

Juliana took the flower and laughed as she watched him move farther down the street. She stood in front of a sidewalk café and when a waiter approached and said, "Here is a table, *señorita*," she sat down to watch the dancers.

A horse-drawn wagon loaded with grapes started down the street. Pretty young girls wearing beautifully embroidered gowns and flowers in their hair stood in each corner of the wagon, smiling and throwing big bunches of grapes down to the crowd. Most of the people seemed to be from the town, but as the wagon moved on Juliana saw people who were obviously tourists among the crowd.

The waiter brought her a small carafe and glass. He poured the white wine and said, "To your health, *señorita.*"

Juliana smiled as she raised her glass. Suddenly, on the outer fringes of the crowd, she saw Brian McNeely—tall, unsmiling, overpowering. He wore jeans that fit like a second skin around his long legs, a white shirt with rolled-up sleeves and a sweater knotted over his broad shoulders. He looked out over the crowd, his dark blue eyes searching every face, frowning as though he didn't approve of the levity.

Juliana pushed her chair back and he saw her. She froze, caught by the anger in his eyes, unable for a moment to move. But when he started toward her she rose, turned and ran through the crowd.

Frantically she fought her way through the throng of people, murmuring, "I'm sorry. Excuse me. Please let me through." A fat man with a handlebar mustache caught her around the waist. When she struggled to get away from him he bestowed a drunken kiss on her cheek and laughingly let her go. She darted a glance over her shoulder. Another man grabbed her. She put one hand against his chest, shoved him out of the way and ran, past dancing couples and costumed prancers, away from the noise and the crowd, down a darkened street. Behind her she could hear his running footsteps.

Fear rose in Juliana's throat as she looked around for a place to hide. Ahead of her she saw the beach. Without hesitation she ran toward it, hoping to hide among the boats. She felt the sand under her feet. Another moment. Another...

A hand grabbed her shoulder. She tried to spin away and felt her dress rip. Brian yanked her toward him and she saw the raw anger on his face. She tried to break free, but his grip was strong and hard as he held her shoulders.

"Stop it!" Brian said between clenched teeth.

"Let me go!" Juliana tried to fight him, tried to break free, but it was impossible. She kicked out, connected with a shin and heard his muttered oath.

"Cut it out!" Brian ordered. "Or so help me...!" He gripped both of her wrists in one big hand and said, "It's over, give it up. I've come to take you back and there isn't a damn thing you can do about it. You can come along with me or you can be locked up in the hellhole they call a jail down here until I can arrange transportation back to Brazil and then home."

Juliana looked up into his angry face. "Let me go," she whispered.

Brian loosened his grip, but his eyes simmered with anger as he loomed over her. "Where's Martinez?" he snarled.

"Emilio?" She looked at him, surprised by the question. She hadn't even thought of Emilio since she'd been in San Benito.

"Don't play dumb, Julie. I know you're here because of him. It only surprises me that it doesn't seem to bother you that he might be involved in your brother's murder."

"Emilio wasn't involved in Tim's death," Juliana protested. "I've said it over and over; he was with me the night Tim was killed."

"And how many nights before and after? After he helped set up Tim's murder?" Brian tightened his hand around her wrists once more. "What kind of a woman are you, to turn your back on your brother's memory and run after a bastard like Emilio Martinez?"

Brian pulled Juliana close to him, so close that she could feel his breath on her face. "Where is he?" Brian demanded. "Where's Martinez?"

"I don't know!" She tried to get away from him. "You're hurting me!"

He let her go. "I know that Martinez sent for you, so tell me where he is and we'll get this over with."

"He didn't send for me. I came to San Benito because of Maria, Tim's wife. She called me and she sounded frightened. I tried to tell that goon you sent to see me that I thought Maria was in danger, but he wouldn't listen. He said Maria was probably a revolutionary too and that he didn't give a damn what happened to her."

Brian frowned. "Bellows is an imbecile," he said. "He didn't say anything to us about Maria. Have you seen her? Where is she now?"

"I don't know." Juliana took a step away from him and rubbed her wrists. "She told me to check into the Hotel Carmen and that she'd call me there. But it's been three days and she hasn't called. I haven't left the hotel, except for tonight. I'd like to go back there now, in case she's trying to reach me."

But Brian shook his head. "You're coming with me," he said. "I'm taking you back to my hotel."

"Your hotel? No, I..." Juliana took a deep breath. "Look," she said. "I promise you that—"

"You promise me?" Brian laughed in a harsh, unpleasant way. "I wouldn't trust your promises as far as I could throw both you and your boyfriend." He took her hand and started up the beach. "You're going to stay with me so I can keep an eye on you." He looked down at her and frowned. One shoulder of her dress was ripped where he'd grabbed her. "Fix your dress," he snapped. "I can't take you into the hotel looking like that."

Juliana stared at him. She'd expected anger but not this...this animosity. She'd liked Brian McNeely when she met him six months ago—almost too much. His kisses had rocked her right down to her toes, frightening her with an intensity of feeling she'd never experienced before. That's why she'd backed off. She and Brian McNeely were too different; she was a free spirit and he was the establishment. She wouldn't even dream of having a relationship with him. But she hadn't forgotten the way he made her feel. Apparently he had.

Brian's legs were so long that Juliana had to almost run to keep up with him. But she knew better than to ask him to slow down. He circumvented the street of revelers in front of her hotel as he headed down the beach past the larger tourist hotels. At last he stopped in front of a small guest house.

"The woman on the desk will be asleep now, so keep quiet when we go in," Brian warned. "In the morning I'll explain that you're my wife and that you arrived unexpectedly."

"But I...I can't stay here with you!" Juliana protested.

"You'll stay with me until I find Martinez, and don't think I won't make good my threats of locking you up if you try to get away from me."

"But I don't know where Emilio is. I don't even know where Maria is." Juliana fought for control. "Please, Brian, I'm telling the truth. I haven't seen or heard from Emilio in months."

Brian looked down at her. He wanted to believe her but somehow didn't. "I don't buy your story," he said, "and I'm too tired to argue with you. I've got to get some sleep."

Sleep! Juliana thought. With him? "Just a minute Brian," she started to protest, but he paid no attention to her as he pulled her after him into the guest house.

His room was on the second floor facing the sea. It was a large room with French doors that opened out onto a balcony. A round table and two chairs had been placed in front of the open doors. The other furniture consisted of a dresser, two nightstands, and one big four-poster bed.

Juliana looked at the bed as Brian released her. "Where am I supposed to sleep?" she asked.

"On the bed with me," Brian said. He kicked off his shoes, unknotted the sweater from around his neck, and loosened his belt. Gesturing toward the bathroom, he said, "The facilities are in there."

Juliana just looked at him, hands on her slender hips. Then without a word she turned and stamped into the bathroom. She turned on the light and glared at herself in the mirror. She'd never met a man like him. Thank God she hadn't let herself fall for him six months ago. He was as mean as a rattler and twice as dangerous. He was brutal, callous and unfeeling, and if he thought she was going to sleep with him he had another think coming. She'd sleep on the floor before she'd get in bed with him.

He was lying on the bed wearing only pajama bottoms when Juliana came out of the bathroom. He got up when he saw her and said, "Take your shoes off, and anything else you want to."

"I'm not going to take anything off," Juliana snapped.

"Suit yourself." He reached for the tie hanging over one of the posts and said, "Give me your hand."

She put her hands behind her back. "What are you going to do?"

"I'm going to tie our wrists together." Brian took a step toward her. In a flat, no-nonsense voice he said, "I'm very tired, Juliana. I spent all last night flying. Today I looked for you. I haven't slept in twenty-four hours and if I don't get some sleep I'm going to be out on my feet. I could handcuff you to the bed but I don't want to hurt you. It'll be easier if we're tied together." He looked at her. "Give me your hand," he said again.

Juliana wanted to defy him. She wanted to tell him she'd rather be tied to the bed than to him. She wanted to fight but she knew she'd be no match for him.

He stepped closer, reached behind her and took her hand. He tied one end around her left wrist, the other around his right. Without a word he led her to the bed. Together they lay down. He pulled a sheet over them and reached to turn out the bedside lamp.

Darkness covered the room.

"I'm a light sleeper," Brian said. "If you move or try to get free I'll hear you."

Juliana didn't answer him. The white curtains moved with the breeze blowing in from the sea. The back of his hand was cool against hers. She felt the tenseness of his body, and of her own. He sighed; after a little while she heard his steady breathing and knew that he slept.

But Juliana didn't sleep. She lay listening to the sound of the waves against the shore, wondering how she could escape from the man who lay beside her.

Chapter 3

Brian opened his eyes, disoriented, unsure for a moment where he was. He felt the breeze and when he turned his head he saw the curtains move and heard the low growl of the ocean. He stretched, then, startled by a murmur of protest stopped and glanced to his right. His eyes opened wide as he stared at Juliana Thornton. She lay on her side with her right hand under her chin and her face resting close to his shoulder. Her tousled red hair tickled his bare chest.

He took a deep breath and tried to steady himself as he studied her face. He told himself she wasn't beautiful, at least not classically beautiful. She was pretty... well perhaps more than pretty. There was something about her, a quality he'd never seen in any other woman. Her smoldering sensuality was touched by an almost waiflike vulnerability that had excited

him from the moment he'd met her. There were faint
shadows under her closed eyes. Her full lips were
gently curved and slightly parted. The torn shoulder
of the dress that he had ripped when he'd grabbed her
last night was folded back to reveal a wisp of lace that
covered one gently rounded breast, a breast that rose
and fell with each breath. Brian tried to look away and
couldn't, even when he felt a stirring of desire. She was
beautiful and he wanted to touch her. He wanted . . .

Juliana opened her eyes. She looked up at him, her
face only inches from his. She didn't move; she
scarcely breathed. There was something in the stillness of his face, in the depths of his blue eyes that held
her as much a prisoner as the hand that was tied to his
own. She felt the warmth of his skin against her cheek
and didn't know whether she was afraid—or simply
reluctant to move away from him. If she tilted her chin
their lips would touch. Her gaze dropped to his mouth
and she remembered how it had been that night on the
beach when Brian had kissed her, how the warmth had
spread from his mouth into hers. It was a kiss that had
left her trembling with need. If he'd taken her hand
then and led her farther up the beach to a dark and
hidden place she would have followed gladly.

That had shaken and frightened Juliana. Brian
McNeely wasn't the kind of a man she wanted to fall
in love with. He was the Establishment with a capital
E and she was a rebel—a protester against things she
thought were wrong, a marcher, a thorn in the side of
the fat-cat wheelers and dealers of the world. She'd
never change, never conform. So every time Brian

called she forced herself to say she was busy, because she was both afraid of him and of the way she felt about him. And she was afraid of the way she thought he felt about her.

But she didn't have to worry about that now. Last night he'd looked at her as though she were a stranger—a fugitive from justice, a woman who didn't care that her only brother had been murdered.

Juliana moved away from him and sat up, forgetting for a moment that she was still tied to his wrist.

"Just a minute," Brian said in a voice made brusque by the strange emotions that were churning through him. "Let me untie you." He pulled her hand onto his knees and undid the knot. Her wrist was red and he held it for a moment. It was small, the bones were delicate. He closed his hand around it, then, not looking at her said, "You can shower first."

Juliana pulled her hand away and slid off the bed. At the bathroom door she turned back. "I . . . I need my things," she said, holding the torn shoulder of her dress. "I can't go around like this."

Brian raised one eyebrow. "No, I don't suppose you can. We'll get your clothes after breakfast and I'll tell them at your hotel that you're moving in here with me in case you get any calls." He waited for her to turn and go into the bathroom. When she didn't he said, "Was there anything else?"

"How long . . . ?" Juliana brushed the tumble of hair back from her face. "How long do you plan on keeping me a prisoner?"

"As long as I have to." Brian's expression hardened. "Until we find your Latin lover."

Juliana looked at him. She lifted her shoulders in a sigh, then without a word she turned and went into the bathroom. She felt frustrated, helpless and scared. She didn't like the feelings.

There'd only been one other time in her life when she'd felt that way—during the summer of her fifth birthday. Her parents had taken her and Tim to their grandparents' farm near St. Augustine. She'd loved the farm but had been lonesome because there weren't children her own age to play with and because fifteen-year-old Tim had no time to spend with her.

One evening at dusk she saw Tim slip out of the house with the single shot .22 rifle his father had given him for Christmas. Juliana had heard Tim and two other boys talking about a possum hunt. She had no idea what a possum hunt was, but she was determined to be a part of it, so she'd followed Tim to the edge of the woods. She'd hesitated there because even in the daytime the woods were a dark and forbidding place. Spanish moss hung from the huge old oak trees like floating wisps of forgotten ghosts, and the silence was almost a living, breathing thing.

After a little while she couldn't see Tim anymore. At first Juliana had been more angry than frightened, indignant that he'd go off this way without her. But when the darkness closed down upon the woods and she began to see strange figures in the swaying Spanish moss she'd started to cry. She turned around and headed back—but she had no idea where the farm was.

She remembered hearing that if you were lost you were supposed to hug a tree. But these big oaks with their ghostly gray Spanish moss weren't huggable. She wandered until she was so exhausted she couldn't take another step. Then she sank to the ground, head on her knees, scrunched up into a tight little bundle of misery and tears.

Tim found her. He held her while she shook and shivered and sobbed on his shoulder, and he carried her back to the safety of the farm.

Tim. For the first time since his death Juliana broke down. She dropped her clothes on the floor, stumbled to the shower, and stood under the pouring water, hanging on to the wall for support, letting the grief come, grief she'd tried to hold back for the sake of her parents and Maria and Rafael. She cried until she couldn't cry anymore. Then she turned the water off, and when she had dried and dressed she went out into the room to face the man who had been Tim's friend, the man who was now her enemy.

"I ordered breakfast," Brian said, indicating the table by the open French doors. "It came a few minutes ago. It'll be cold if we don't..." He stopped. Juliana's eyes were red and swollen from weeping. He looked at her, feeling awkward and uncertain. He wanted to go to her, to put his arms around her and tell her that everything was going to be all right. Instead he said, almost accusingly, "What's the matter? Are you ill?"

Juliana shook her head. "No, I . . . I was thinking about Tim." She turned her face away. "I didn't cry at the funeral," she said miserably. "Maria and my mother and father were so devastated. Somebody had to hold things together. But now . . . I don't know." She looked up at Brian, then away. "Tim and I didn't always get along, especially in the last few years. He was a lot like you, I guess. And I'm . . . I'm not. But all of a sudden I remembered another time, a time when I was very young and frightened and lost, and Tim found me." Her eyes filled with tears again and she looked away. "I saw you at the funeral. I'm sorry I didn't get a chance to speak to you, to thank you for coming."

"Tim was my friend." Brian scowled. "He was your brother, Julie. I can't understand why you insist on sticking to your story that Martinez spent the night with you on the night Tim was murdered."

Juliana put down the cup of coffee she'd just picked up. "I didn't say that Emilio spent the night with me. I said we had dinner together that night." Her gaze met his across the table. "There is a difference, you know."

"Is there?" Brian added cream to his coffee, and without looking at her said, "Where is he, Julie?"

She shook her head. "I don't know."

"Damn it!" Brian hit the table with his fist and saw her flinch. Trying to control his anger he asked, "How did you and Martinez meet?"

"Maria introduced us."

"Maria?" He looked surprised.

"Emilio is her cousin. When he came to Miami she gave a party for him and I was invited. We started dating."

"How did Tim feel about it?"

"He didn't approve." A ghost of a smile turned up the corners of Juliana's lips. "But he didn't really approve of anybody I went out with."

"Or of you."

She looked startled, then with a sigh she said, "Poor Tim. He just didn't know what to do with me. Did you know that he'd bailed me out of jail the afternoon of the night I met you? I'd been at a sit-in against a manufacturing company for dumping chemicals into the Miami River. Tim was giving me the silent treatment and I was so mad I wore that crazy outfit to show him I didn't give a damn." Her face sobered. "But I did . . . give a damn, I mean. I hated it when Tim disapproved."

"But that didn't ever stop you from doing what you wanted to do, did it?"

Juliana shook her head. "No, Brian. I'll always fight for what I believe in."

"Or for who you believe in?" His voice was bitter. He looked out at the sea, then back to Juliana. "Tell me about Maria," he said.

"What do you want to know?"

"What she's like. Tim met her here in San Benito, didn't he?"

Juliana nodded. "He said he was sitting by the swimming pool, sipping a piña colada and minding his own business when a vision in a white bikini walked by. He started talking to her, took her to dinner that night, and two weeks later they were married.''

"How did you feel about that? Did you like her?''

"Of course I liked her, in spite of the fact that she's the most beautiful woman I've ever seen.'' Juliana smiled, then her face sobered. "She made Tim happy, Brian, she softened him. When Rafael was born I thought Tim would burst with happiness.''

Brian nodded. "I remember,'' he said. "He passed out cigars and told everybody who'd listen that Rafael was the most perfect baby who'd ever been born and that Maria was the most beautiful and the bravest woman in the world.'' He refilled Juliana's coffee cup, then his own. "What about her family?'' he asked. "Do you know anything about them?''

"Not much. They raise tobacco, I think. Maria said they have a farm, the Quinta Espinosa, about an hour's drive from here. I thought that if I didn't hear from her by today I'd rent a car and drive out there.''

"We'll do it this afternoon.'' Brian stirred his coffee. "You said she introduced you to Martinez. Why did Tim object to your dating him?''

"I don't know. He said Emilio was too suave, that his hair was too slick and his mustache was too thin. Dumb things like that.''

"Tim knew about people. He could spot a crook a mile away.''

"Emilio's not a crook!'' Juliana glared at Brian across the table.

"So you're still in love with him." Brian's eyes glittered with anger. "That's why you're protecting him, isn't it? That's why you came to San Benito."

"I came to San Benito because Maria wanted me to come and because of your Mr. Bellows's insinuations that I had anything to do with all this. Emilio disappeared the day after Tim was murdered and I don't know where he is." Juliana took a deep breath. "Please," she said, "please believe me."

Brian looked at her. He wanted to believe her, to believe that the innocence and the vulnerability he saw in her face were real. The still-damp red hair curled softly around her shoulders, and he wanted to reach out and touch her because she looked as fresh and as clean as a summer morning. Maybe she was telling the truth. Maybe it was all over with Martinez. Maybe she didn't know where he was.

Outside Brian could hear the rush of waves breaking against the shore. He looked away from the deep magic of Juliana's eyes, took her hand and pulled her to him. "I'm going to take a shower," he said. "I have to make sure you don't try to run away from me."

Juliana looked at him, then away. For a moment she thought Brian had believed her. She'd thought she'd seen something in his eyes, a softening, a remembrance of the way it had been between them that night on the beach. But she'd been wrong. There was no softness in Brian McNeely, no memory of a kiss that had left her shaking with need.

Without a word she let Brian lead her to the bed. He handcuffed her wrist and put the other cuff around the thinner part of the bedpost, just below the knob that would keep it from sliding off. She sank down on the bed and closed her eyes.

When he came out of the bathroom he was dressed in gray slacks and a black polo shirt. He briefly glanced at Juliana, stepped into black loafers, and picked his money up off the dresser. When he released her he said, "Don't try to run away, because you won't be able to. But if you do try I'll handcuff you to me. Is that clear?"

"Quite clear." She gazed up into his eyes and knew that he would do what he said.

They left the area near the ocean and started inland, toward Juliana's hotel. The streets were still crowded with revelers, some of them wide-awake, some of them looking dazed from last night's wine and lack of sleep. Brian held Juliana's hand as they walked past closed shops and cafés filled with people. A middle-aged couple jostled against them. The man, bald, perspiring and obviously drunk, looked at Juliana, whistled, and tried to pull her away from Brian. Brian stepped between them to shoulder the man away. The man, protesting that this red-haired angel was the woman of his dreams, put his arm around Juliana's waist and attempted to drag her away while his wife sputtered something in Spanish. Brian finally lifted the man off his feet and deposited him on the sidewalk.

Juliana waited, grinning in spite of herself. Then, through the crowd of amused onlookers, she saw Emilio Martinez.

He was seated in the café they had just passed and he had turned, as other people had, to watch Brian carry the now loudly protesting man to the sidewalk. Emilio saw her and rose to his feet, his black eyes wide with surprise. He quickly shook his head.

Juliana froze. She opened her mouth to say his name, then stopped. She had to talk to him alone before Brian saw him. She had to find out both why he'd disappeared and if he'd had anything to do with Tim's murder. If she told Brian that Emilio was here there wouldn't be time for questions. He would arrest Emilio and take him to Miami to stand trial. She couldn't let that happen, not until she knew for herself that Emilio wasn't involved.

Brian came striding angrily to her. "Do you always have that effect on men?" he growled.

"Only on Tuesdays." Juliana flashed him a smile and saw his look of surprise. She felt both frightened and elated. Emilio would help her get away from Brian, then together she and Emilio would find Maria and Rafael. She made herself look at Brian, away from the street, away from Emilio.

When they approached the Hotel Carmen, Juliana deliberately slowed her pace. If Emilio was behind them, she wanted to give him time to follow her. She paused a moment or two with the desk clerk when she asked for her key, then together she and Brian stepped into the elevator to the second floor.

As they walked down the hall to her room, Juliana began to plan how she could get away from Brian, what excuse she could invent to get him into the bathroom or the closet, lock him in and find Emilio. For the first time since she'd arrived in San Benito Juliana felt a surge of hope.

She handed Brian the key to her room. He unlocked the door, held it open for her to go first, then stepped inside.

What took place next happened so quickly that Juliana could barely take it in. Emilio stepped from behind the door, arm raised, a stone twice the size of a baseball clutched in his hand. She gasped, frozen. Brian turned to look at her with a puzzled expression.

"What?" he started to say just as Emilio brought the rock down against his head.

Brian fell without a word. Emilio pulled Juliana into the room and slammed the door behind her.

"Pick up your things," he said. "We've got to get out of here."

Juliana looked at Emilio, then dropped to her knees beside Brian. A knot had already formed on the side of his head and a thin trickle of blood was running down his temple. She reached for his wrist. His pulse was weak but steady; his face was paste-white. She looked up at Emilio, at the solid, square body and the handsome face, but before she could speak Emilio yanked her to her feet.

"We've got to get out of here, Julie," he repeated in a low voice.

"But Brian... We can't just leave him here," Juliana protested. "He's hurt, he needs a doctor. He—"

"I didn't hit him that hard." He shoved Juliana toward her closet. "Pack your things, just what you need for a couple of days." He leaned against the door, listening. "The maid's coming," he whispered. "Hurry!"

"But, Emilio..." She looked down at Brian. "I can't leave him. Not like this."

"Julie, please!" He hurried past her to the closet, pulled out one of her suitcases, and began throwing her clothes into it. Then he snapped the case shut and coming back to her said, "The maid will find him, Julie. He'll be all right." And when she shook her head he said, "I've come to take you to Maria, Julie. She and Rafael are in trouble."

"Maria?" Juliana looked at him, then down at Brian. They heard the maid knock on the door next to theirs.

"Julie, please, we've got to get out of here!"

She swallowed hard, then with one desperate last look at Brian, let Emilio lead her to the door, out of the hotel, and into his waiting car.

Chapter 4

The scream awoke Brian. He opened his eyes and saw a woman with a gray cap bending over him, hands to her face, eyes wide with fright and shock.

"Please don't scream," he managed to say. He put a hand to the back of his head, felt the bump and the moistness of blood, and struggled to a sitting position. What in the hell had hit him? What...? He looked for Juliana, realized she wasn't in the room, and felt a terrible flash of fear. My God, what had happened? Where was she? He shook his head, but it was hard to think because of the pain racketing around inside his brain. The maid had stopped screaming. She ran into the bathroom and came back with a wet cloth and held it to the back of his head.

"*Gracias,*" Brian said. "Thank you, I'm all right. Did you see a young woman when you came in?"

"No, *señor*. Not in the room. I saw a young woman and a man leaving just before I made up the room next door."

"A man? She left with a man?"

"*Sí, señor*. A man of your age, but not as tall as you. He looked to be from San Benito."

Brian closed his eyes, wincing with pain and with the thought of what Juliana had done. "Did she... Did it appear that he was forcing her to go with him?"

"Forcing her? No, *señor*. She went willingly."

"I see." Brian pulled himself to his feet and staggered to a chair. "Thank you very much for your help. I'm all right now."

"Would you like me to call the police, *señor*?"

"No, that won't be necessary."

"If you want anything just ask at the desk for Consuelo."

"I will, and thank you."

When the woman went out the door, Brian leaned back in the chair and closed his eyes. He tried to reconstruct what had happened since they'd arrived at the hotel. They'd stopped at the desk for Julie's key, then they'd gone upstairs and he'd unlocked her door. He rubbed a hand across his face, trying to remember what had happened then. She went into the room and he stepped in after her. Then what? Suddenly Brian stiffened and it seemed to him he could see her face as it had been at that moment—shocked, frozen. He'd wanted to ask why but it was too late. He'd felt a sickening thud of white heat in his head and everything had gone black. He hadn't seen who'd hit him, but she had. And she hadn't warned him.

The thought of that sickened Brian as much as the pain in his head. For a while this morning he'd almost believed her when she said she'd come to San Benito to find Maria, not because of Emilio Martinez. Now he knew what a fool he'd been. It was Emilio who'd been waiting for him behind the door and Julie had known he was there. She'd stood by while Emilio hit him, and then she'd just left him there.

Brian sat looking out at the sea for a long time. When the pain and the dizziness began to recede he got up and went into the bathroom. He took two aspirin, then got in the shower and let the cold water beat against his body. All the while he tried not to think of Julie and what she had done.

"Where is Maria?" Juliana asked as Emilio headed the car out of the city.

He glanced at her. A muscle in his jaw twitched. "She's in the mountains."

"Are she and Rafael all right?"

"Of course. San Benito is her home, Julie. No harm can come to her here."

"But why is she in the mountains? Is that where her family's farm is?"

"No. The farm is called Quinta Espinosa, and that's where we're going now."

"But you said we were going to see Maria and Rafael." Juliana turned in her seat and glared at him. "I want to see them," she said angrily.

"We will see them," Emilio soothed her. "But first we must go to the Quinta." He covered her hand with his. "Trust me, Julie."

Trust him? She stared at Emilio for a moment, trying to see beyond the good looks, past the black curly hair and the dark Latin eyes. He was an intelligent, charming man, and she'd done her best to fall in love with him, partly because she really liked him and partly because Tim disapproved of him. He'd sent her white roses, and almost every time he came to pick her up he brought a small gift—a stuffed animal, chocolates, a book he thought she'd like. On their last night together he'd brought her a book of Spanish poems.

He was an easy man to fall in love with, but she hadn't, and when she saw that his intentions were serious she'd broken things off—the night they went to Key Biscayne for dinner—the night of Tim's murder.

"But I love you," Emilio had said. "I'll be patient, Julie. In time I'll make you change your mind. Don't shut me out of your life. Let me be your friend, for now." He'd been sweet and sad and he'd kissed her such a tender good-night that she'd almost changed her mind.

Juliana had been hurt and puzzled that he hadn't called or tried to see her after Tim's death. He had simply disappeared. She'd been shocked this morning when she'd seen him. Her one thought had been that he would know where Maria and Rafael were. He would get her away from Brian. Then she'd looked up at Brian, so tall and fierce and angry and she'd felt a clutch of pain because she didn't really want to leave him. It was almost as though the thought of leaving him was dishonorable.

Juliana closed her eyes and tried to block out the memory of his face and the questioning look in his eyes just before the stone came down. As long as she lived she'd never forget the way he looked at her in that last moment before he fell. She'd left him. Oh God, she'd left him lying there because Emilio had said he'd take her to Maria.

She turned her head and looked at Emilio. "Why did you run away?" she said. "Why did you disappear after Tim was killed?"

He reached for her hand. "There were... circumstances, darling. I had to leave." He took a deep breath. "I love you, Julie, but there are things a man must do, a conscience of the heart that a man must follow when his country is involved."

"What are you talking about?" Juliana demanded. "How dare you talk about conscience of the heart? My brother was murdered and the next day you disappeared. I don't want to hear about your country or the things that a man must do. What does that have to do with Tim's death? What did *you* have to do with Tim's death?"

"Nothing." Emilio tightened his hand on hers. "I swear to you, Julie, I had nothing to do with that. You must believe me, darling."

Juliana stared at him for a moment, then she pulled her hand away and moved over on the car seat as far as she could. Hot air blew in the open windows. Vine-covered trees with low-hanging branches and untrimmed brush grew close to the winding road. Soon the vegetation gave way to fields of sugarcane. Beyond the cane fields lay the mountains. They drove past small huts with clothes drying on front yard bushes. She smelled woodsmoke and roasting corn, and tried not to look down at the three-thousand-foot drop on her side of the car. She tightened her hands in her lap and closed her eyes to block out the memory of Brian lying unconscious and helpless, the trickle of blood showing starkly against his pale face. She'd never forget the way he'd looked, or the terrible wrench of pain she'd felt when she left him.

When Emilio pulled off the road Juliana looked at him inquiringly. "We're almost at the Quinta," he said. "We'll talk then and I'll explain everything." He reached for her hand again but she pulled away from him and turned her face to the window. In the distance she saw the house and the other buildings surrounding it. It was a big, Spanish-style dwelling, gleaming white against a rolling green lawn. Beyond the house lay a grove of trees.

Emilio parked in front of a garage. "We're here." He opened his door and then came around to open hers. He looked at Juliana, hesitated, then said, "There'll be others inside. I want you to be careful of what you say."

Juliana looked puzzled. "When are we going to see Maria?"

"Later. I'll take you to her later." A step sounded behind them. Emilio whirled around and when he saw the man who had approached he said, a shade too hardily, *"Hola, Francisco. ¿Como estás?"* He put a protective arm around Julie.

The man was in his middle fifties. He had a three-day growth of beard, a shaggy mustache and scraggly chin whiskers. He wore an unbuttoned khaki shirt over a sweat-stained undershirt, khaki pants that were belted low over his hips, and straw sandals. He held a rifle in the crook of his arm.

"You brought the woman," he said in Spanish. With a wave of the rifle he indicated the house. "The others are waiting inside."

Emilio's hand tightened on Julie's arm and for the first time she felt a chill of fear. Who were the others? Countrymen of Emilio's? Terrorists? Revolutionaries? What had they done to Maria and Rafael? What did they want with her?

Emilio picked up her suitcase and led her through a patio to a long corridor. An elderly, grim-faced woman, dressed in a maid's uniform, opened the door before Emilio could knock. *"Buenas tardes,"* she said. "The other gentlemen are in the library." She looked at Juliana, frowned when she saw the torn dress, and said, "She should change before she meets them."

"That's a good idea, Esperanza. Would you be kind enough to show Miss Thornton to her room?"

The woman picked up Juliana's suitcase. "This way," she said, indicating that Juliana was to precede her.

The room Juliana was taken to was beautifully appointed. Sheer mauve curtains matched the bedspread and blended with the flowered pink chaise lounge. There was a dresser, a dressing table, a small desk, and wooden, Spanish-style bars on the floor-to-ceiling windows.

The woman looked around the room, then went out and closed the door. The lock clicked.

So she was a prisoner. Thoughtfully Juliana opened the suitcase. She looked at the dresses that Emilio had so hastily thrown in, and at the high-heeled pumps, not quite sure what one wore when facing one's captors. What one wore, she decided, was something one could run like hell in if the opportunity arose.

Fifteen minutes later, dressed in designer jeans, a long-sleeved pink-and-white-striped shirt and sneakers, Juliana knocked on her door. The woman opened it immediately and told Juliana to precede her down the hall. When they reached the library the woman knocked once, then opened the door and motioned Juliana inside.

The four men who had been seated rose to their feet. Emilio, standing beside a large stone fireplace, came forward to take her hand. "Gentlemen," he said, "may I present my fiancée, Miss Juliana Thornton."

Juliana looked at him in surprise, but before she could speak he led her to a silver-haired man, the oldest person in the room, and said, "Juliana, this is Señor Ricardo Zamora. The two gentlemen on his right are Miguel Otero and Javier Gallo." Emilio paused, then indicating a handsome man in his mid-forties said, "This is Alejandro Espinosa."

"Espinosa?" Juliana's eyebrows rose in question. "You're Maria's brother?"

"Her cousin, Señorita Thornton, as are Emilio and Señor Otero. Maria has told me much about you, but her words don't do you justice. I don't believe I've ever seen hair quite your color. It's magnificent."

"Where is Maria?" Juliana said, ignoring the flowery compliment. "I want to see her."

"All in good time," Ricardo Zamora said smoothly. He took Juliana's arm and led her to a high-backed, brocaded chair. "Is your room comfortable, Señorita Thornton?"

She nodded. "It's a splendid room, Señor Zamora, the most beautifully appointed jail I've ever seen."

"Jail?" One delicate finger stroked his perfectly trimmed mustache. "My dear *señorita*, you are our guest. Haven't you heard the Spanish saying, *Mi casa es su casa*? My home is your home. We want you to consider the Quinta Espinosa your home while you're in San Benito."

"Most homes don't have bars on the windows, Señor Zamora. I feel like a prisoner and I am a prisoner. I want to know what's going on."

"Julie, please," Emilio implored her.

"I told you she'd be difficult to manage," the man named Otero said angrily. "You should have taken her up to the cabin with Maria and the kid. If she stays here she'll only cause trouble."

"Shut up!" Emilio exploded. "Just shut up!"

"Who will make me, *cabrón*?"

"Gentlemen!" Ricardo Zamora held up his hands. "Sit down and let us try to discuss this calmly." He turned to Juliana. "Would you care for a glass of sherry?" he asked. "We have some amontillado from Spain. It's a bit on the dry side but—"

"No, I don't want a glass of sherry." Juliana's voice rose to a shout. "I want to know why you've brought me here and I want to know where Maria and Rafael are!"

"We brought you here—we convinced Emilio to bring you here—because we wanted to become better acquainted with you," Zamora said.

She turned and looked at Emilio. "You... you... brought me here, knowing I'd be a prisoner," she sputtered angrily. "You lied to me; you said you were taking me to Maria!"

"Darling, please..." Emilio's expression was distressed. "I had to get you away from McNeely. I—"

"McNeely?" The small, dark man whose name was Javier Gallo jumped to his feet. "McNeely's here?"

"He arrived yesterday," Zamora said. "Miss Thornton spent last night with him in his hotel room." He looked at Juliana. "That's true, isn't it?"

"Yes, it's true," Juliana snapped. "But I was his prisoner, just as I'm your prisoner now." Emilio stepped forward to place his hand on her arm, but she shrugged him away and turned to face Alejandro Espinosa. "I came with Emilio because he told me he'd take me to Maria and Rafael. I don't understand any of this. I don't know whether you're terrorists or revolutionaries and frankly, I don't give a damn what you are. All I want to do is find Maria and Rafael and get the hell out of San Benito!''

"She's working with McNeely," Otero said. "Find out what she did with the book and get rid of her." He turned on Emilio. "It's your fault, Martinez. You've risked the cause, everything we've been fighting for because of her. You gave her the book, damn you. You—"

"Because there was no other way." Emilio faced the other man. "I've told you, I've told Zamora, if the police had caught me with it we'd have been finished."

Juliana looked from Emilio to Otero. The book? What were they talking about? Did all of this have something to do with Tim? With his death? Dear God, these were the men responsible for Tim's death. For a moment the thought, now the certainty, that Emilio had been a part of Tim's murder sickened her to the point of nausea. Then the nausea passed, to be replaced by an anger so deep it took every bit of her control to keep from flying at Emilio. She wanted to hurt him as profoundly as he'd hurt her. She bowed her head and clenched her hands together to keep her anger in check. She could do nothing against five men. She had to wait, to bide her time and hopefully escape.

The conversation went on around Juliana. She wouldn't answer any of their questions. She accepted a sherry and later, when dinner was served, she forced herself to eat. When the meal was finished, Señor Zamora said, "We will talk about this tomorrow,

Señorita Thornton." He took her hand, bowed and kissed it. "We're not terrorists," he said. "We're honest men who love our country and want her to be free. Perhaps our methods are hard, but we must fight against tyranny any way we can."

Juliana looked at him, then her gaze flicked to the other men in the room, finally resting on Emilio's face. "Even if it means killing," she said in a low voice.

Emilio's shoulders tensed. "I must talk to her alone," he said to Zamora.

"Not tonight." The older man's voice was firm. He touched a buzzer that lay on the table beside him and waited until he heard a knock on the door. "Come in," he said then, and the maid, Esperanza, entered.

"Take Señorita Thornton back to her room," he said. "Make sure that she is comfortable and if there's anything she requires get it for her."

Esperanza grunted. Her quarterback's hand fastened around Juliana's arm as she hustled her out of the door. It was dark now and candles glowed from wall sconces along the outside corridor. Beyond the lights everything was dark. When they got to the room, Esperanza took a ring of keys from the pocket of her uniform. She inserted one of them into the lock, opened the door, and propelled Juliana inside. A lamp burned on the table beside the bed.

Without a word Esperanza started to close the door.

"Just a moment." Juliana's voice was imperious.

The maid glared at her. "Well?" she said.

"When I bathed before dinner I couldn't turn the faucet off in the bathtub. Would you try it, please? I won't be able to sleep if the faucet's dripping."

"Too bad about that." Esperanza glared at her.

"Señor Zamora said if I required anything you were to get it for me." Juliana took a step forward and with the same kind of expression she'd used when she'd stood up to the head of the biggest manufacturing company in Florida, said, "I can't sleep while a faucet is dripping. If you refuse to fix it I'll tell Señor Zamora that you treated me rudely. I don't think he'll like that."

Esperanza's expression hardened, but a look of uncertainty shadowed her eyes. She put the ring of keys on one of the chairs, grunted again and marched into the bathroom. Juliana was right behind her. She stood in the doorway. "It was the hot water tap," she said.

"It doesn't appear to be dripping." Esperanza leaned over the tub and turned the offending faucet with one beefy hand.

"It was this afternoon." Juliana stepped into the room, dashed forward, and before Esperanza could move, she shoved as hard as she could against the woman's solid back, then sprang back, slamming and locking the door behind her.

A muffled groan came from the bathroom, but Juliana knew that as soon as the woman recovered the cry wouldn't be muffled, it would be loud enough to send everyone in the house running. She had to run first.

Cautiously Juliana moved to the bedroom door and opened it. She looked out. The corridor was empty. She went back and picked up the keys off the chair, slipped out of the room, locked the door and dropped the keys behind a pot of flowers.

She thought she remembered seeing a stand of trees to the right of the house when they'd driven in today. She made her way along the corridor toward the front door. From the library she heard a voice raised in anger and she flattened herself against the wall, scarcely daring to breathe. Quickly she ran out to the patio, staying in the shadow of the overhanging plants until she reached the iron gate.

Just as Juliana reached it a voice cried out, "Who is it? Who's there?" and she knew it was Francisco, the guard with the rifle. Dropping to the ground, she crawled to the bushes growing at the side of the driveway, and lay without moving.

He called out again and Juliana heard him coming toward her. He kicked at the bushes, his boot narrowly missing her body. "Damn cats," he muttered. He leaned against the gate, only inches from where she was. She heard a scratch, then saw the flare of a match and smelled the burned sulfur and tobacco.

Juliana held her breath and closed her eyes, waiting. Finally, after what seemed an eternity, he moved away. Again she waited, making herself stay where she was in spite of her cramped position. Ten minutes went by. Fifteen. Cautiously she stood up and looked around. The night was silent. Then, like a roll of thunder, the roar of a Valkyrie split the night air. Esperanza had come to and was calling for help.

There was no time for caution now. Juliana ran toward the trees. Behind her she heard a shout. She raced on. She had to reach the cover of the woods before they saw her!

Then suddenly the trees loomed before her, as dark and forbidding as the trees on her grandparents' farm so long ago. For one breathless second Juliana stopped, then she plunged into their darkness. Panting for breath, she paused a moment, trying to get her bearings, then ran on. She didn't see the figure that moved out from behind one of the trees until it jumped in front of her. It grabbed her and she screamed.

"Shut up!" the man growled.

Juliana gasped, trying to see a face through the darkness. "Brian?" she whispered. "My God, Brian, is it you?"

"Yes, damn it." His hands tightened on her arms. "Don't try to get away from me, Julie. I—"

But Juliana wasn't trying to get away. Instead she flung herself into his arms and buried her face against his chest.

"Brian," she said over and over again. "Oh, Brian." And clasped him in her arms.

Chapter 5

Juliana didn't ever want to move. She just wanted to stay here, close to Brian, feeling the thump of his heart against her ear and the warmth of his body next to hers.

As for Brian, all sorts of emotions were churning inside him. He didn't understand Juliana. She'd left him unconscious to go with Emilio. Now she was clinging to him as though she'd never let him go. What in the hell kind of a woman was she? What in the hell was the matter with him? Because suddenly, here in this jungle of trees with a bunch of revolutionaries hot on his trail, all he could think about was the way Juliana's hair smelled and how warm and soft her breasts felt against his chest.

With a supreme effort, as angry with himself as he was with her, Brian held her away from him.

"Where's Emilio? What happened? Why were you running away?"

"Because he's one of them." Juliana shuddered. "They're revolutionaries or terrorists or..." She tried to get a grip on her emotions. "There are four of them, besides Emilio, and a guard. The guard almost caught me." Her hands gripped the front of Brian's shirt as though she was afraid he might try to get away. "A maid who's built like a Sherman tank locked me in a room with bars on the windows. I tricked her into going into the bathroom, and I shoved her in the bathtub and locked the door and that was her you probably heard yelling a minute ago." She looked up at him and tried to steady herself. "I'm sorry, I know I'm babbling. Are you all right?"

"No, I'm not all right. I've got a bump the size of a tennis ball on the back of my head and the worst headache I've ever had in my life." Brian gripped her arms and shook her hard. "You knew someone was there, didn't you? You—"

A shout rang out. Then Francisco yelled, "She headed for the trees."

"It's the guard," Juliana whispered.

"Let's get out of here." Brian grabbed her hand and pulled her after him, holding one arm out in front of him as he crashed through the trees. They ran blindly, stumbling over roots. Once Juliana fell. He yanked her up, hissing, "Move, damn it!"

Then suddenly they were through the trees, out in the open—vulnerable and exposed. Ahead of them lay another stand of trees, but to reach it they'd have to cross an open stretch of almost three hundred yards. The shouts grew closer.

"Run!" Brian said as he sprinted forward.

Juliana strained to keep up with him, and she did, but by the time they reached the shelter of the trees she was gasping for breath and her side was cramped with pain.

"Wait . . ." She fought to get her breath. "Brian, I can't . . ."

"You damn well can!" His hand tightened on hers and he started to run again, almost dragging her after him.

Juliana tried. She gave it everything she had but it wasn't good enough. She tripped and fell and lay trying to suck air into her tortured lungs. Before she could speak Brian picked her up and slung her over his shoulder. Then he was off and running through the bush, with her body bouncing against him like a sack of potatoes. If she'd had any breath left it would have been jarred from her.

"Put me down!" she managed to gasp.

"Shut up!" he said in a low growl.

"I won't!" She struggled to break his grasp. "I—"

He silenced her with a firm hand over her mouth. She heard cries behind them and knew that Francisco and the other men were gaining on them. Suddenly Brian stopped. Juliana raised her head and saw that they were at the foot of a rocky cliff. He set her on her feet. "We've got to climb," he whispered as he hoisted her up onto a rock. "Get a handhold. That's it, up you go."

Juliana climbed. She grabbed whatever she could reach to pull herself up, the limb of a tree, a rock, and when she didn't move fast enough Brian shoved her from behind. When they heard voices they flattened themselves against the rocky surface. A beam of light shot up from below. It searched to their right, above and below them. Juliana pressed her face against the rock. Below her Brian put a steadying hand on her ankle, holding her still, comforting her with his touch.

When the voices faded they climbed on. Juliana had never known that a night could be so dark. Something skittered past her once. She stopped, muffled a cry, then swearing under her breath, dug her nails into the rock once more and inched upward.

The voices returned just as they slid over the ledge of the cliff onto a softness of grass.

"Wait," Brian cautioned. "Don't move."

Move? Who could move? Juliana lay on her back, eyes closed, gasping for air. She was aware of Brian beside her and knew that he had crept closer to the edge to peer down through the darkness.

"I don't think they're going to come up here," he whispered at last. "Come on." He helped Juliana to her feet and led her toward a grove of pines. Fifteen minutes later he said, "We've lost them," and sank to the ground. He rested his head against a tree and looked at Juliana. "Are you all right?" he asked.

"Battered, bruised and breathless, but yes, I'm all right." Juliana lay down beside him, then hitching herself up on one elbow, looked at Brian. "Why are they after us?" she asked. "Why did they lock me up?

I don't understand. Emilio and I were friends. He's Maria's cousin.'' She shook her head. "I don't understand any of this."

Brian tried to see her face through the darkness. "It was him in your hotel room, wasn't it? He's the one who hit me."

Juliana held her breath. "Yes, Brian, but I didn't see him until it was too late. I didn't know he was there."

"And I suppose you didn't know he was in San Benito?"

"No, I didn't, not until today. I...I saw him just after that nutty man wanted to waltz me around the square." She sat up and put her hand on Brian's arm. "But I didn't know he'd be waiting for us in the hotel room. I didn't know he'd hit you."

"Didn't you?" Brian's laugh was harsh. "You went with him, Julie. You didn't give a damn whether I was alive or dead. All you cared about was that your lover had returned."

"That's not true," she protested. "I went with him because he told me he'd take me to Maria. He said she and Rafael were in trouble. I didn't want to leave you, Brian, believe me, I didn't."

"Believe you?" Brian turned away from her and stretched out. Gruffly he said, "We'd better try to get some sleep. They'll be after us again in the morning."

Juliana looked at his closed and angry expression. With a sigh she sank down on the pine needles. Her body was stiff with tension. The night was still and dark as she looked up through the branches at the stars. She was terribly aware of Brian beside her, of the rise and fall of his chest, of the strength of his arms and the length of his body. She closed her eyes. The scent of pines filled the air and the earth was cool beneath her back. She wanted to touch him, to reassure herself that he was there, but knew that she dare not.

The night grew cold. From somewhere above an owl hooted. She inched closer to Brian. Her arm touched his and she felt him stir. Something moved in the grass nearby and she clutched his hand.

"What's the matter?" he growled.

"Something moved." She hated the fear in her voice. "An animal. Maybe a snake."

Brian listened for a moment. "I don't hear anything. Go back to sleep."

"I haven't been to sleep. I can't sleep without a pillow."

"Oh for...!" Brian glared at her, then pulled her to him so that her head rested in the hollow of his shoulder. "Will this help?"

Juliana nodded against his chest. "Thank you," she whispered.

Brian didn't answer her. He didn't move. He told himself he would not put his hand on the back of her head and soothe her to quietness. He tried to ignore the warmth of her body, her faint womanly scent, the press of her breasts against his side. He remembered the night on the beach when he'd kissed her, when for the briefest of moments she had melted against him. A fire burned in his blood and he felt his body tighten with need.

Juliana murmured sleepily and with a sigh burrowed closer. He swore under his breath and she put her arm across his chest.

"Julie? Damn it, Julie," Brian whispered.

She moved her hand on his chest, burning her brand across his skin, and it was too much. It was past bearing. With a low groan he grasped her chin and turned her face to his. Her eyes flew open. An exclamation rose from her lips but Brian stopped them again, this time with his mouth. He felt her surprised resistance, but he didn't stop. He couldn't stop.

Brian kissed her with all the anger and passion he'd kept bottled up these past two days, with all the hunger and the longing that had haunted him the last six months. He rolled her onto her back, his hands clasped on either side of her head, and ground his mouth against hers, forcing her lips apart. He felt her startled gasp, then her tongue danced to meet his and she answered his kiss with all the fire and the passion he'd remembered.

Brian's lips were hard against hers. He nibbled the corners of her mouth and took her lower lip between his teeth to bite and suckle. Her lips felt swollen, but she offered them to him, relishing the feel of his mouth on hers.

Juliana's fear of the night was forgotten as she gave herself up to the demands of his passion. With trembling hands she undid the buttons of his shirt to feel the heat of his skin. He groaned and she felt him tear her shirt in his eagerness to touch her. When he pushed the straps of her bra down and began to kiss her shoulders, Juliana curled her fingers through the thickness of his brown-gold hair and raised her body so that he could unfasten the front hook. But when he exposed her breasts she tensed, remembering the fierceness of his kisses.

But there was no fierceness in the hands that caressed her. With the utmost gentleness Brian ran his thumbs across the peaked tips before he bent to kiss them. His breath was warm against her skin, his lips were tender.

Passionately she whispered his name. But mingled with the desire in her voice was a note of fear, a fear he didn't heed because he'd passed the point of pulling back. It didn't matter that she'd belonged first to Emilio Martinez. He'd make her forget. With the seduction of her body he'd wipe away the memory of any man who had gone before him.

Brian sat up. He pulled her shoes off, tugged the jeans down over her hips, and yanked at his own clothes.

"Brian?" Her voice was tremulous. "Brian, I..." But he stopped her words with another kiss that left her shaking with a need that matched his own and lifted himself over her.

"Look at me, Julie," he said hoarsely, then claimed her.

Juliana gasped with pain. Brian froze then began to speak, but Julie put a hand against his lips, then caressing his shoulders, urged him closer.

He couldn't hold back then. He moved against her, carefully, slowly. Only when Juliana raised her body to his did he thrust deeper. He clasped her in his arms, his body covering and enveloping her, shaking her to the roots of her being.

Suddenly a sensation Juliana had never before experienced surged through her, blinding her to reality, frightening her with an intensity of feeling she'd never thought possible.

"It's all right, Julie." He drew her closer in his arms. "It's all right, love."

"But I...oh, Brian..." She looked up at him, then beyond to the night sky as the stars exploded into a million pieces of white fire. She cried his name into the darkness and heard his own primitive answer.

Brian gathered her into his arms, his face against hers as he held her, still too filled with the passion of what had passed between them to speak. He felt the trembling of her body and kissed the side of her face.

It was a long time before either of them spoke. At last Brian said, "Why didn't you tell me you were a virgin, Julie?"

"I didn't expect the question to come up."

"I hurt you." He tightened his arms around her. "I'm sorry. I had no idea. I thought you and Martinez...?" He let the question hang in the air.

"No," Juliana whispered.

Brian raised himself on his elbow and looked down at her. With a slight grin he said, "I thought you were such a liberated woman, a rebel who did whatever she wanted to do and to hell with what anybody thought."

"I am a liberated woman," Julie protested. "In my own way. But not...not that way."

"I see." Brian kissed her. Then he put his hand on the back of her head and held her and thought what a strange and wonderful creature she was. She nestled against him and he felt his heart expand with a feeling that he didn't quite understand. In a little while her breathing evened and he knew that she slept.

But Brian didn't sleep. He only held her and listened to the night sounds and knew that when she awoke he would make love to her again.

The sun filtering down through the trees woke Juliana. She felt the softness of pine needles under her and heard the exultation of larks in the trees above. She turned her head and saw Brian looking at her.

"Good morning, Julie." He kissed her nose. "Did you sleep well?"

She felt hot color flush her cheeks. "I...yes, thank you." Her voice was stiff and formal. She didn't know what to say. What *did* one say on the first morning after?

Brian's hand rested on her naked waist. Her eyes flicked over his chest, lower, then quickly back to his face. "Well," she said, trying to make her voice hearty, "I suppose we should get going."

"I suppose we should." Brian didn't move. His hand caressed the line of her hip and slid around to her bottom.

"I wonder if there's anything to eat around here."

"I doubt it." He pressed her closer to his nakedness. And when she stiffened in his arms he said, "I know all this is difficult and strange for you, Julie. I'm sorry that I hurt you last night." He smoothed the tumbled hair back from her face. "But I won't hurt you again, Julie. Believe me, I won't."

Brian's lips found hers to gently brush away the harshness of last night's kisses. He caressed her breasts and she shivered with pleasure. When he eased himself over her, she remembered the pain and tried to hold back. But Brian wouldn't let her. He kissed her again as he grasped her hips and slowly, carefully entered her.

Suddenly Juliana's fears were forgotten. She clasped Brian to her and answered his kiss as a wonderful warmth enveloped her. She became more aware of the world around her, of the scent of the trees and the slick feel of pine needles under her back. She burrowed her face against Brian's neck and smelled the man-sweetness of his skin.

He went slowly, stroking easily and gently so he wouldn't hurt her. She opened her eyes and looked up at him and he was lost in the dark depths of her eyes and in the softness that surrounded him.

Juliana lifted her body to his. Her lips parted and her cinnamon eyes were smoky with pleasure. A look of wonder passed over her beautiful face and she cried out as passion shook her once again.

His own body exploded then in a rush of feeling unlike anything he'd ever known before. They held each other, close and warm, with the morning sun filtering down through the towering pines.

* * *

"I want to know about the men who were at the Quinta," Brian said. "Do you remember their names?"

They were dressed now, sitting cross-legged under the trees, eating mangoes that Brian had found in a nearby tree. Juliana took a bite out of hers and leaning back against the trunk of the tree wrinkled her forehead in concentration. "The man who seemed to be in charge is named Ricardo Zamora. He's in his late fifties or early sixties and he's distinguished looking. His clothes looked tailor-made and expensive." She raised an inquiring eyebrow. "Have you ever heard of him?"

"Yes, I have. He was President Sanchez-Fuentes's secretary of defense until the attempted coup. When the coup failed he joined the rebels and for the last two years he's helped organize the guerrillas. He's determined to overthrow Sanchez-Fuentes. What about the other men?"

"One of them was Maria's cousin. His name was Alejandro. He's good-looking, with the same dark hair and green eyes as Maria. And there was a Javier somebody and a man named Miguel...Miguel Otero, I think. He's Maria's cousin, too."

Brian whistled. "I've heard of him. Every revolution has somebody like Otero. He's the guy who doesn't mind doing the dirty work when it has to be done. The others, the men like Emilio and Ricardo Zamora consider themselves patriots. They're men who love their country and tell themselves they only do what they must do, kill if they must kill, in the name of freedom. But men like Otero do it because they like to kill. They..."

The color drained from Juliana's face. Brian put a hand on her arm and felt her trembling.

"Was it Otero, or somebody like him, who killed Tim?" she whispered. "Is that what Tim's death was all about? A revolution here in San Benito? Oh, my God, Brian, do you think Emilio used me to get to Tim? Did I help kill my own brother?"

"Of course you didn't." Brian pulled her into his arms. "Not any more than Maria did."

Juliana pulled away from him. "Maria? What are you talking about?"

"She's a part of the Espinosa family, Julie."

"What are you saying?" Her voice rose in disbelief. "That she was a part of Tim's murder? A part of the men who killed him?"

"No, of course not. I don't doubt that Maria loved your brother. But her family's involved, Julie. They're revolutionaries. They've been trying to overthrow Sanchez-Fuentes for years." Brian hesitated, wondering how much to tell her. "That's what Tim was working on when he was murdered," he said at last. "He'd been trying for months to get a line on the revolutionaries and how they operated."

Juliana looked at him. Her face was pale with shock. "Tell me," she said faintly. "Please, Brian, tell me what you mean. How Maria's family is involved."

Brian took a deep breath. "Tim and Maria were married two weeks after they met, Julie. They didn't know anything about each other except that they were in love. Tim had come to San Benito for the government because word had leaked out that there was going to be an attempted coup. The name Espinosa didn't mean anything to him, he was in love with Maria and that was all that mattered." Brian ran a hand across his two-day beard. "He didn't tell Maria what he did until a month after they were married. Tim said when he did she was so furious she locked him out of their bedroom for a week."

Brian got to his feet. His expression was thoughtful, and for a moment he didn't speak. "I don't suppose any woman really wants to make a lifetime commitment to a man in our kind of work. At first Tim thought that was why she was upset; it was only later he found out about her family's connection to the rebels in San Benito."

"But Maria couldn't... She wouldn't have done anything to hurt Tim!" Juliana protested.

"No, I don't think she would have. But it must have been hard on her, loving Tim, loving her family and believing in what they believed." Brian looked down at Juliana. "Maria must have been pretty upset when you started dating Emilio."

Juliana swallowed hard. "Tim was the one who seemed more upset by it," she said quietly. She looked away and her throat tightened with anguish. "I don't even think I'd have gone out with Emilio a second time if it hadn't been for Tim. We'd been at odds for so long about so many things. He disapproved of everything I did. He hated it when I took part in protests and I thought he was square and establishment and..." She covered her face with her hands and began to weep for her dead brother and for all the times they had fought and argued and hadn't loved each other.

Brian dropped to his knees beside her. He pulled her hands away from her face. "Tim loved you," he said. "He loved your fighting spirit and your bravery. Even when he was angry with you he was proud of what you were doing, Julie." He put a finger under her chin and forced her to look at him. "I saw Tim in the office the night I met you. He'd just come from bailing you out of the Dade County jail. He was mad as hell for a little while. He thumped his desk a couple of times and he said, 'Why does she do it, Brian? If there's a cause she believes in, she'll fight for it even if it means ending up in jail. She's been a rebel since the day she was born.'"

Brian wiped Juliana's tears away with his thumb. "He told me he was ten years older than you were, and that when you were little he thought you were a terrible pest. He said he'd yell at you and try to order you around and that you'd put your hands on your hips and yell right back at him." Brian chuckled. "You must have been some kid," he said. "Tim told me that once, when you were five or six, he spanked you for breaking an Elton John record. He said he turned you over his knee and you bit him, damn near to the bone." Brian tilted her face up. "Tim told me he never laid a hand on you again and that he would have killed anybody who did."

Brian kissed her. "He was proud of you, Julie. He was proud of your courage, of your free and wonderful spirit, and he loved you. Believe me, he loved you."

He leaned back against a tree and held Juliana while she wept. He thought of the child she had been, of the girl she had grown up to be, and of the woman she was now. The thought that maybe he was falling in love with her more than worried him—it terrified him.

After a little while he eased her from his arms and said, "We can't stay here all day, it's time to get moving."

But when she left his embrace his arms felt curiously empty.

Chapter 6

It was late that afternoon when they found the village of Tenango near the foot of the volcano.

"That's Manitura," Juliana said. She looked up at the towering peak almost hidden by clouds. "Maria told me about it. She called it the sleeping volcano."

"Was it ever active?"

Juliana nodded. "She said a few centuries ago it was, but that now it just rumbles once in a while to remind everybody that it's there."

Brian looked up at the misty peak. "That's what they said about Krakatoa and Mount Saint Helens." He took Juliana's arm. "Come on, let's see if we can get something to eat."

Tenango was a small village. There was a post office, a marketplace, two cantinas and an open-air restaurant where they ate heaping plates of tamales, and

scrambled eggs laced with chili. After they had cooled
their mouths with cold beer, Brian asked the waiter if
there was a hotel or a guest house where they might
find a room for the night.

"There is no hotel, *señor*," the waiter said as he
cleared their dishes, "but old Gaspar sometimes rents
one of his *palapas*, his beach huts." The man glanced
at Juliana. "They are picturesque and one is only a
few steps from the sea, *señor*, but I don't think they
would do for the *señorita*."

"They'll do." Brian handed the waiter some money.
"We'll find this Gaspar down at the beach?"

"*Sí, señor*. Tell him Antonio sent you."

"I will, Antonio. *Gracias*."

They went to the marketplace to buy food, tooth-
brushes, soap and other items before they headed
down to the beach. Juliana had run away from the
Quinta with only her handbag and she desperately
wanted to change from her soiled and torn shirt into
something fresh and clean. While Brian bought what
supplies they might need, Juliana went in search of
clean clothes. She found a red Spanish-type peasant
blouse that would look fine with her jeans, and after
she had paid for it wandered among the other stalls.
She paused when she saw a stall of dresses and cotton
nightgowns. The woman selling them said, "The
nightgowns are handmade, *señorita*."

Juliana picked one up. It was white, old-fashioned
and prim looking. The high neck and long sleeves were
trimmed with lace.

"I'll take it," Juliana said.

She thought of last night and this morning and of what it had been like making love with Brian. She was joyously glad that there hadn't been anybody before him, and if that was a hopelessly medieval attitude then so be it. She'd held herself in check for years, infuriating every man who'd desired her, denying all of the feelings that sometimes left her shaking and miserable. She'd waited for somebody like Brian. For Brian.

Juliana looked past the market stalls, searching for him through the crowds. When she saw him she smiled. He was so big, well over six feet, and powerfully built. His shoulders were football-player wide, his waist and hips were narrow. His face was strong— the nose blunt, the jaw square and solid. But his well-formed mouth, and the eyes that were as blue as the sea, saved his face from harshness. He was not a classically handsome man, but he was rugged and masculine. Juliana didn't think there was a woman alive who wouldn't look at him with speculation in her eyes.

But she and Brian had nothing in common. They were too different to even think about a permanent relationship. He was like Tim; he had *establishment* stamped on his forehead. For him the law was the law and right or wrong he would uphold it. She wouldn't, not always, not if she disagreed.

She'd been terribly attracted to him the night they met, which was why she'd refused to see him for two weeks. Finally she'd given in, just to prove to herself that she couldn't possibly be interested in a man like Brian McNeely. She'd watched him during dinner that night, watched the play of light across his strong face, the way he curled his fingers around his wineglass. She'd looked at his mouth and thought that soon he would kiss her. He had, of course, and it was everything she remembered—it had also terrified her. She'd backed away and refused to go out with him again.

But she hadn't forgotten him. Even when she'd started dating Emilio, she'd only thought of Brian.

At the beach they found Gaspar Rodriguez, a short, stout man with a round face and a fringe of white hair circling his otherwise bald head. He told them that all the *palapas* were available, but they were most humble dwellings and he was not sure the *señores* would like them. But of course there was nothing else in all of Tenango and if they wanted a place it would have to be one of his huts or nothing.

"I'm sure one of your *palapas* will do quite well," Brian said.

Señor Rodriguez led them down the beach to a row of bamboo huts set among the palm trees. The roofs were made of palm fronds, the floors were sand. They stopped at the last hut, a distance from the others, and looked inside. It was simply furnished, with a low table and two stools, a few dishes, a pan and bowl, and two *petates*, straw mats, on the sand.

"There's drinking water at a stand near my hut," Rodriguez said. "The facilities are there, also."

"It will do." While Brian paid him, Juliana stepped inside. Brian chatted with Rodriguez for a moment, then ducking his head, he entered the hut and stood looking around before he said, "Be it ever so humble..."

Juliana's smile was cheerful. "The ocean is right at our front door. It will be wonderful tonight..." She blushed. "I mean—"

"I know what you mean." Brian drew her close to him. "You're right, Julie. It *will* be wonderful tonight."

They bought a fish from a fisherman, and that night Brian built a fire on the beach. While he cooked the fish Juliana prepared a salad of the tomatoes and onions and avocados she'd bought at the market. They brought the small table outside and ate there in the darkness of the night with only a thin slice of new moon and the smoldering fire to see by. The sound of the waves lulled them, and when they had eaten Juliana leaned back against Brian's shoulder and closed her eyes. She knew there were things they needed to talk about. They had to find Maria and Rafael and there was still the danger that Emilio and Ricardo Zamora were looking for them. But they would think about that tomorrow. She would enjoy tonight, and she would always remember it.

She was almost asleep when Brian said, "How about a swim?"

"Mmm, that sounds wonderful, Brian. But I don't have a suit."

"You don't need one." He turned her face up to his. "There's no one on the beach, Julie. We're alone and it's dark. There's no one to see us."

"But I've never...I mean I..." She hated herself for stammering like a ten-year-old.

"Another never?" Brian laughed deep in his throat. "You're a paradox, Julie. You come off as a liberated woman of the eighties but a part of you is still in the 1900s."

I love it, he thought. I love being the man she first made love with, the man she'll swim in the nude with. He thought then of all the things he would teach her, of all the ways he would make love with her. And because he knew that if he didn't stand up they would make love right there on the sand, he got to his feet and pulled her up beside him.

"You've got exactly two and a half minutes to take off your clothes," he said.

"But—"

"Two minutes." Brian grinned as she ran into the hut and he began to take his own clothes off. When he was naked he went down to the water's edge to wait for her. She came hesitantly out of the hut and he felt the breath catch in his throat. She was so beautiful. She stood before him, glistening in the moonlight, slim and finely made. He could see the rise and fall of her breasts as she came toward him and he didn't move until she was beside him.

Brian touched her shoulder. Then he kissed her very gently, took her hand and led her into the water.

They swam parallel to the shore, then drifted and let the waves carry them together. Brian kissed her, a wet, salty kiss, with his tongue warm against hers, his arms against her back, holding her close as for a moment they sank beneath the water, wrapped in each other's arms. He pulled her to him and she could feel his masculine strength pressing hard against her nakedness.

They rose to the surface and Brian kissed her again, kissed her until she trembled and swayed closer. His chest was hard against her breasts. Her body felt swollen with need.

"Julie," he whispered against her lips. "Oh, Julie."

When they swam back to shore they stopped in the waist-deep water. He put his hands on Juliana's shoulders and slowly slid them down to her breasts. He heard her indrawn breath and ran his thumbs across her peaked nipples, bending and kissing her with a hunger that left both of them shaking with need. With a hoarse cry he swept her off her feet and carried her to their hut. Gently he laid her down on the straw mats.

"You're so beautiful," he said as he smoothed her hair back from her face. "I want you, Julie. I want you so much." He eased his body over hers and felt the wet coolness of her skin against his. For a moment he only held her, then kissed her parted lips and with a sigh he entered her.

Juliana slipped her hands around his bare back as she rubbed her face against his shoulder and raised her body to his. She could hear the rustle of palm fronds and the roll of waves against the shore, and it seemed to her that they were alone in this island paradise. She thought of all the people who had gone before them, of lovers who had made love on straw mats on nights like this, of whispered sighs and yearnings. Then Brian kissed her and there were no more thoughts, only feelings.

His movements were luxuriously slow. He rained kisses over her face and her breasts and carried her higher and yet higher on a crest of feeling she would not have thought possible. When her body tensed and the breath rasped in her throat he slowed his movements. "Not yet, love," he whispered. "It's too good, Julie, too good to end." He tightened his hold on her body, rocking her to him as he began to move again.

Juliana threaded her fingers through his hair. She lifted her body to his, wanting to please him, wanting to be whatever he wanted her to be, to do whatever he wanted her to do. But oh, what a sweet agony this waiting was. Her body cried out for that final moment and she pulled his face to hers and kissed his hungry mouth with all the fervor of her passion.

It was too much—for him, for her—and with cries of joyous desperation they soared to that final peak of ecstasy.

"I'll never let you go," Brian whispered as he clasped her to him. "You're mine now, Julie." His body shook with reaction. "You belong to me."

Juliana tightened her fingers on his shoulders. Touched by the intensity of his voice, by the strength of his big body over hers, and by her own trembling slide from passion, she said, "Yes, darling, I'm yours."

Brian sighed against her lips. In a little while he rolled so that her body rested on his. "Sleep, love," he said. Then he stroked her sea-damp hair and her back and held her until he felt her relax and heard her even breathing.

But it was a long time that night before Brian slept. He knew they couldn't stay there, that Zamora would be looking for them. Guerrillas all over the island would be given the word that a United States government man and the woman who had once been Emilio Martinez's girlfriend were dangerous to the cause of the revolution and must be apprehended. Tenango was a remote village, but word would soon reach here, too. They had to leave, but oh God, he wished they could stay forever. Just himself and Julie, alone in this rustic hut with the sound of the waves and the rustle of wind in the palms.

Brian was alone when he awoke the next morning. He lay for a few minutes, warm and lazy and content, then got up and looked out. Juliana, dressed in a white nightgown, was sitting on the sand in front of the hut, looking out at the sea. He looked at her for a moment, and when he spoke her name she turned, smiled at him, and stood up. The sun was behind her and he could see the lines of her body through the thin fabric. She was barefoot, and looked very young and innocent in the prim, high-necked gown. Her red hair, loose over her shoulders, turned to fire in the morning sun.

When she took a step toward him Brian's heart stood still. Something close to a sob rose in his throat because he knew he'd never seen anything quite as lovely as she was at that moment.

"Good morning," she said. "Isn't it a beautiful—" But Brian took the words from her lips. He kissed her slowly and passionately, savoring the taste of her lips before he picked her up and carried her inside the *palapa*—their *palapa*.

Brian laid her down on the straw mat. He removed the gown and folded it and placed it on one of the stools. He knelt beside her. He brushed her fiery hair back from her face and ran his hands down her naked body, marveling in the texture of her skin, the lines and curves of her. He came back to kiss her lips and when he had sampled and tasted them, he lifted her hands above her head, holding them there while he kissed her raised breasts.

Only when she pleaded with him did he let her go. He began then to trail warm kisses down her body, rubbing his beard-roughened face against the smooth skin of her stomach, then soothing it with his lips. He ran hot kisses over the curve of her hips down to her thighs. Gently he bit the delicate skin there. When Juliana put her hands on his shoulders to draw him away he grasped her hips and kissed the tender skin again before she could move.

Juliana whimpered in protest and struggled to break free, but even as she protested wildfire shot through her veins and her body trembled with a feeling she'd never known before. She was frightened, but mixed with her fear there was an excitement and a feeling that drove all sense of reality from her mind. She was helpless against the passion that shook her body, that made her cry out a mindless litany of his name.

He shifted his body over Juliana then, joined himself with her and rocked her to him. He carried her higher and still higher on a crest of impossible pleasure, until finally, trembling, pulsating with one last moment of ecstasy, they fell back to the safety of each other's arms.

"I love you," Brian said as he kissed her damp brow. "I think I've loved you since the night we first met."

Juliana looked up at him. Her eyes were smoky brown, her trembling lips still swollen from his kisses. "And I love you," she whispered. And knew that for as long as she lived there would never be another man in her life but Brian McNeely.

When they swam in the sea that afternoon Juliana wore her torn shirt over her panties; Brian wore his shorts. They came out of the water to buy fresh fish and fruit from a local vendor, and cold beer from Gaspar. After Brian rebuilt the fire they brought the straw mats from the hut and spread them on the sand, sitting opposite each other while they ate.

Brian knew they should leave as soon as they finished. It was madness to stay there another day. He looked at Juliana, at the way the sun reflected on her face and the way the wet shirt clung to her breasts. Her legs were long and shapely, the ankles so slender he could circle them with his thumb and forefinger. Just a little longer, he told himself. One more afternoon, one more night here in this tropical Eden with my Eve, my Julie.

They walked along the beach that afternoon. They swam, and made love, and swam again. When night fell they sat for a long time looking out at the sea, silent and a little sad, because they knew without having spoken of it, that tomorrow they would leave.

When the hour grew late Brian stood and helped Juliana to her feet. He put his arms around her and kissed her. Suddenly the sand beneath their feet quivered and shook. Juliana looked up at Brian. She held tight to his shoulders, and trying to joke she said, "That was some kiss."

"It sure was!" He grinned at her. "I wish I could tell you that's what caused the ground to shake, but I can't. I'm afraid it was the volcano."

"Oh, God. It wouldn't really erupt, would it?"

Brian kissed her again. "Of course not."

But that night the earth shook again and they heard the threatening rumble of the sleeping volcano. As they slept the flames leaped up, bright orange against the slender slice of moon.

"Do you have any idea, any clue at all, as to where Maria and the boy might be?" Brian asked the next morning.

Juliana shook her head. "All Zamora said was that Maria and Rafael were at a cabin in the mountains. It probably belongs to the family."

"That doesn't give us much to go on. Did they say anything else? Anything about anything?"

Juliana thought for a moment. "No, I don't think so. They..." She looked stricken. "Oh, damn," she said. "Of course. Otero said something about a book. He was angry with Emilio and he said, 'You gave her the book.'"

"What book? What was he talking about?"

"I don't know, Brian. Emilio often gave me little presents: roses, chocolates, a book now and then."

He glowered at her. "A really romantic guy, right?"

"Right." Julie lifted her chin. "He'll make some woman a terrific husband, but not me, okay?"

Brian nodded, but he still looked angry. "What about the book? What kind of a book?"

"I don't have any idea, Brian. He gave me two or three in the six months we dated. The night before he disappeared he brought me a book of Spanish poetry. Maybe that's the one they were talking about." She looked at him, frowning. "What's in it, do you think?"

"Maybe the names of other revolutionaries, or of their connections in the States. Maybe their gunrunning routes. I think Emilio knew he had to get away, that there was a chance he'd get caught. He didn't want to get caught with the book on him so he gave it to you." Now it was Brian's turn to frown. He didn't want to frighten her, but he thought she'd better understand how serious the situation might be. "It's possible Zamora thinks you know more than you do, Julie. That could be dangerous for you. Maybe that's why they're holding Maria and the boy, to get to you through them."

"We've got to find them, Brian. There must be other Espinosas here in San Benito. We could try to find them and ask if they know anything about a family cabin."

"Anybody with the name Espinosa is probably mixed up in the revolution. We can't take that chance." Brian put his arm around her shoulder. "I haven't wanted to say anything, but I think Zamora and Emilio are out looking for us right now. We've got to go back to the city."

Juliana nodded. "We can go ask the police for help."

Brian shook his head. "We can't do that. San Benito's on the verge of a revolution and we don't know how many people are involved."

"You mean even the police might be?"

Brian nodded. "It's certainly a possibility." He hesitated, and putting his hands on her shoulders said, "When we get back to town I'm going to put you on a boat and send you to Belém, then back to Miami. I want you where I know you'll be safe."

Juliana stepped away from him. There was a hint of anger in her eyes when she said, "I'm not going to leave San Benito without you and Maria and Rafael. I know you don't like Emilio, Brian, but whatever he's involved in, whether it's gunrunning or a revolution, I know he wouldn't do anything to hurt me."

"You don't know anything!" Brian's voice was angry. "Damn it, Julie, you're going to do what I say about this. You're going back to Miami."

Juliana pulled away from him. "Maria's my sister-in-law," she said, "and Rafael is my nephew. I'm not going anywhere until I know they're all right."

"You'll do what I tell you to do."

Defiantly she took a step closer to him. "Who made you king of the island?" she demanded.

He glared down at her. "I'm going into the village now," he said between clenched teeth. "I'll arrange for transportation back to the city. And when we get there I'm going to find a boat and you'll get on it."

"No, I won't!"

Brian's expression reflected his anger. This morning she'd looked like an angel in her simple white nightgown, vulnerable and delicate, a young woman who needed taking care of. Now suddenly she'd reverted to the rebel who'd picketed the Turkey Point nuclear plant and been arrested for a sit-in at the electric company. How in the hell did you handle a woman like this?

"I'll be back in a little while," Brian said. "Be ready to leave."

Juliana glared at him, then stalked down to the water and without looking back swam straight out.

How dare Brian tell her what to do? She wasn't going to leave San Benito without Maria and Rafael—and without him—no matter what he said. She had no intention of letting him get away with ordering her around just because they'd made love.

Juliana rolled onto her back and looked up at the cloudless blue sky. She'd never known, hadn't even imagined that making love would be so wonderful, so shattering. She'd always prided herself on being completely in control of her emotions, but when Brian made love to her she wasn't in control. Her body took wing and zoomed to heights she hadn't even dreamed of. It was exciting and wonderful, but she didn't intend to marry a man who would tell her what to do and when to do it. She would have to keep her distance and never make love with Brian again.

With a groan Juliana flipped over and began to swim. Who did she think she was fooling? She couldn't back away from Brian—she loved him. He'd been right when he said she belonged to him, just as he belonged to her. But how in the world would she ever get along with him?

He had disappeared by the time she returned. She went down the beach to where Gaspar had rigged a shower and washed her hair. Then she went back to the hut and dressed in her jeans and the red peasant blouse she'd bought at the market.

Thirty minutes later Brian returned with a canvas bag for their belongings and fruit he'd brought for the trip. "There's a bus back to the city," he said. "It leaves in fifteen minutes."

Juliana nodded without answering. When they turned away from the hut she paused and looked back. It looked alone and deserted. A rush of tears flooded her eyes. This had been their paradise, their particular slice of heaven. She didn't want to leave.

"Come on." Brian's voice was impatient. He turned and saw the tears. For a moment he didn't speak. Then he said, "This place will always belong to us,

Julie. When this is over we'll come back and it will be like it was." He tilted her face to his. "I promise you, love. I promise we'll come back some day."

He kissed her then, and didn't notice that the sand moved beneath their feet and that smoke began to belch from the mist-covered peak of Manitura.

Chapter 7

They went first to Juliana's hotel. Brian waited for her while she packed and checked out, then he took her to his place on the beach. "As long as you're in San Benito I want you where I can keep an eye on you," he told her. "Tomorrow morning I'll try to find a boat to take you to the mainland."

Juliana's face was set and angry. "You can't force me to go if I don't want to, Brian. And I *don't* want to. I came to take Maria and Rafael home with me; I'm not going back without them."

Brian could feel his temper rising again. "I've told you," he said evenly, "I'll find them."

"They're my responsibility. Rafael is my god-child." Juliana hesitated. She wanted Brian to understand the special relationship she had with the child. Last year she and Rafael had spent a magical week-end in Disney World and it had been a wonderful revelation for her to see things through his little boy's eyes. The thought of the danger he might be in now, frightened her.

"Rafael is a very special little boy, Brian," she said thoughtfully. "I couldn't love him more if he were my own child. Losing Tim was terrible for him, his whole world turned upside down." Juliana fought to keep the tears back. "Now he's here on this island, among people he's never seen before. He must be terribly bewildered, frightened by all the strangeness. If there is a revolution he could be in danger. I want him out of here. I want him where I know he'll be safe."

"Nothing's going to happen to him, Julie. He's part Espinosa and so is Maria." Brian put his arms around her. "But you're not."

"What . . . what do you mean?"

"You're expendable."

She paled, but before she could speak Brian continued. "These people are revolutionaries, Julie. They're desperate to overthrow a dictator-type government. A whole new way of life, for them and for future generations, depends on whether or not they succeed in what they're doing. One man—or one woman's death—is of little importance if that man or that woman stands in the way of their cause.

"These are desperate men, Julie, who won't let anything or anyone stand in their way. You've been in danger from the moment you set foot in San Benito and I want you out of here." Brian put his hands on her shoulders. "Look at me," he said. "If anything happened to you I'd never forgive myself. I have to know that you're safe, Julie, that's why I'm sending you away.''

"But *I* have to know that Maria and Rafael are safe. I can't go back until I know they are."

"Damn it!" In a voice made rough with anger and frustration Brian said, "Haven't you heard anything I've said? We're in the middle of a revolution. The men involved are dangerous, they—"

"Emilio wouldn't do anything to harm me, Brian."

"He may not be able to help himself." Brian shook his head. "You're getting out of here tomorrow if I have to tie you up and put you on the boat myself." His face hardened. "If I have to I'll take you back to Belém and have the Brazilian authorities there put you on a plane for Miami. I have the authority to do it, Julie, and don't think I won't!"

Juliana believed him, but that didn't change her determination to stay. She knew that for the moment at least it would do her no good to argue with Brian.

When he let her go Juliana showered and changed to a blue cotton dress that fell low on her shoulders and white sandals. When she was ready she went out to the balcony to wait for Brian. They'd reached an impasse; she didn't doubt for a moment that what he'd said about the Brazilian authorities in Belém sending her back to Miami was true. She'd have to change her tactics. She'd agree to go and while Brian was out making the arrangements, she'd slip away from him. He'd be furious but she couldn't help that. She had to get to Rafael.

When Brian came out to the balcony he said, "I've sent down for drinks. I thought we'd watch the sunset from here."

His expression was careful and Juliana knew he was making an effort to put their argument aside. The drinks arrived and he sat in the lounge chair next to hers. They spoke little as they watched the tropical sun sink in a blaze of color into the sea. As the sky changed from vermilion to flamingo to dusty pink, Brian said, "I want you to get in touch with Jack Kelly as soon as you get to Miami. Tell him what was said about one of the books Emilio gave you. He'll want to see them."

"I still don't understand why Emilio gave me something that was so valuable to the revolution."

"You said he told the others he was afraid of being caught with it. But he made a mistake by giving it to you and Zamora knows it." Brian frowned. "They're probably going to try to get the book back and that means you might not even be safe in Miami."

"Then let me stay here."

"No, Julie. I'll have Jack arrange a safe place for you."

Juliana forced a look of calm acceptance. No, you won't, she decided. I'm not going to Miami, Brian McNeely, and you can't make me.

When they finished their drinks they went to a small seaside restaurant where they sat in a secluded booth gazing out over the water. They ordered cold shrimp that was served with a sauce so hot it brought tears to Juliana's eyes. Brian laughed and held a glass of white wine to her lips. When she sipped the wine he kissed her and tasted the coolness of her lips, the heat of her mouth. He reached under the table to caress her thigh. She looked at him, her lips slightly parted, her eyes suddenly soft with desire.

They ordered lobster and by the time it came the restaurant was almost empty. Brian cut each piece of the luscious meat, dipped it into the hot melted butter, and fed it to her. He licked the buttery corners of her mouth, warming and weakening her with his hand on her thigh.

By the time they left the restaurant Juliana's body felt heavy and swollen with need. She leaned into Brian when he put his arm around her. Soon they'd go back to their room and this anguished waiting would end.

But Brian didn't take her back to the hotel. Instead he took her to a smoky-dark lounge filled with music, and without waiting for a table, led her out to the dance floor.

She and Brian had never danced together. As he put his arms around her, she rested her face against his shoulder and closed her eyes, letting herself drift with the music.

Brian leaned his chin against her hair and breathed in the scent of her. He brushed his fingertips across her bare shoulders and she moved closer. Her back was warm against his hand, and he thought how fragile she was as he felt the small bones of her spine. He heard the faint catch of her breath as he caressed the back of her neck and a small sigh as she nestled closer.

They were wrapped in the drift of smoke and the music. Juliana could feel the strength of his hard body against hers, the movement of his hips, the press of his male arousal. Her body yearned for his, every nerve electrified by his touch. Her skin burned where he pressed his hand against her back. Brian kissed the soft skin behind her ear and ran his fingers across her bare shoulders.

"Julie," he whispered. "Do you know how much I want you?" He closed his arm around her waist, making her painfully, meltingly aware of his desire.

Juliana nuzzled him, nibbling his earlobe, darting her tongue daringly against his skin.

Brian's body shook with need. He kissed her then in a dark and smoky corner of the dance floor, kissed her until she was dizzy and trembling, until her body melted against his and she had to cling to him for support. When he let her go he looked at her for a long moment, then he took her hand and led her off the dance floor and out of the lounge, down the street the few blocks to their hotel.

Juliana was breathless by the time they arrived, filled with a quivering excitement at what was to come, frightened by her own emotions and by the fierce look of sexuality on Brian's face. They went into the room and without waiting to turn on a light he pulled her to him and kissed her. Then he picked her up and carried her to the bed.

Brian kissed her desperately and began to undress her. When she was naked he tore at his own clothes, threw them aside, and covered her body with his. "I love you," he said. "I want you. Now and always, only you."

Juliana gasped as he pressed against her—shocked by the pulsing warmth of him. Her breath quickened and she clasped him to her.

"I love to bury myself into your softness," Brian murmured against her lips. "I'll never get enough of you, Julie. Love, oh my love." He cupped her buttocks with his hands and drew her closer, rocking her to him as his cadence quickened.

She was lost, drowning in a sea of an emotion so primitive that it frightened her. She clung to him as she whispered his name. She dug her fingertips into his arms, holding him as he held her. It was too fast, too soon, this sudden burst of passion that drove all thought, all reason from her mind. Her own voice sounded foreign to her as she cried out his name. He took her cry of passion into his mouth as together, with shattering intensity, they reached the peak of love and tumbled over the precipice.

Brian held her so close she could feel the thud of his heart against her breasts. He caressed her, smoothing back her damp hair and raining kisses on her face.

When they had rested Brian felt himself begin to grow again; he rolled over so that Juliana was on top of him. He lifted her and eased her down to straddle him. He saw the shyness, the uncertainty of her face and felt overcome with love as he touched the sweet roundness of her breasts, caressing the apricot tips. She shivered as she began to move slowly against him.

"Yes, love," he murmured. "That's it, Julie." He closed his eyes. His nostrils fluted with desire as she moved slowly, sensually against him. She felt his body tremble and her own body swelled with the knowledge that she was doing this to him. His hands were warm on her breasts, gently tugging and teasing. I can go on this way forever, she thought. It's wonderful, I don't want to ever stop.

Brian opened his eyes. He put his hands on her hips to guide her movements. Juliana tried to go slowly, to savor this wondrous feeling, but suddenly the feeling turned into a flame that threatened to overwhelm her.

She whispered his name. He slid his hands to her shoulders, pulling her closer so that he could kiss her mouth as the inevitable moment raced nearer and nearer. Juliana surged against him, carried on a tide of uncontrolled need as he lifted his body to hers and whispered his triumphant cry against her lips. Brian told her how beautiful she was and how much he loved her. He soothed her to calmness and held her until she slept.

Juliana lay curled beside him when he awoke. Brian looked at her tousled hair and the memory of the night came flooding back. She'd been quicksilver, fire and lightning, wondrously, vibratingly, passionately alive. And Brian knew that he had awoken this passion in her. There'd been no one before him. That first time she'd been as shy as a young fawn, but last night she'd come into her own as a woman, a woman who demanded even as she gave. He loved that in her, just as he loved her fighting spirit. He wanted to marry her, but he wouldn't fool himself; Julie would be a handful. She was mercurial, a rebel, a will-o'-the-wisp with a mind of her own. She'd never be the kind of wife who'd belong to women's clubs and have the pot roast on the table when he came home. She'd be out marching for whatever cause she believed in, even if it meant spending a night in jail. She'd be many things, but never dull.

Brian gazed down at her. Her lips were slightly parted, there were smudges of fatigue under her eyes. One arm was thrown across his chest, one leg over his leg. He put the palm of his hand against one breast. He took the tip between his thumb and first finger and gently squeezed.

Without moving or opening her eyes, Juliana said, "You're an insatiable fiend." She moved closer.

Brian pulled her into his arms. With his face against her hair he said, "Do you have any idea how much I love you?" He kissed her lips and her breasts and when it became too much for both of them he joined his body to hers.

Afterward they showered together. While Brian phoned down for breakfast, Juliana put on the white nightgown she'd bought in the village. When they finished breakfast, Brian said, "I'm going to call Jack Kelly. I'll tell him you're coming to Miami and about the book Emilio gave you."

"Brian—"

"No arguments, Julie. You're going to Miami and that's final." He got up and coming to her chair leaned down and kissed her. "I'll find Maria and her son, Julie. But I've got to do it my way. I can't travel or do the things I might have to do if you're with me or if I'm worried about your safety. I want you to leave San Benito today."

For a long moment Juliana looked at him. "I came to San Benito because of Maria and Rafael, because they were in trouble and I wanted to help them. I still do, Brian, but they're not the only reason I want to stay." She touched the side of his face. "I want to stay because of you. Because if anything happened to you..." She leaned her face against his shoulder. "Please, Brian, let me stay. I promise I won't be any trouble. I'll do whatever you tell me to do, please don't send me away."

Brian stroked her hair and held her. "I'm sorry, Julie, but the answer is no." He tilted her face up to his and kissed her. "I'm going to call Jack now," he said, "then I'm going down to the docks to find a boat that will take you back to Belém."

She started to speak but Brian put a finger against her lips. "End of discussion, Julie. I want you to pack while I'm gone so that you'll be ready to leave when I get back."

Juliana looked up at him. She knew it wouldn't do her any good to argue. He went into the room and soon she could hear the murmur of his voice on the telephone, her name, Emilio's name. "Right," she heard Brian say. "I'm sending her off the island to-day. She'll call you from Belém when she knows what time her flight gets into Miami. I'd like you to meet her at the airport, Jack."

When Brian finished his call he came out to the balcony. "I'm leaving now," he said. "Lock the door behind me."

"Very well," Juliana said coldly. She didn't look around. She didn't even say goodbye.

She was still sitting out on the balcony when the phone rang. Reluctantly she got up, sure that it was Brian wanting to tell her that he'd arranged for a boat. She picked up the phone. "Yes?" she said.

"Julie? Julie, is that you?"

"Maria? Where are you?"

"Around the corner in a tobacco shop. I don't have much time."

"My God, Maria, I've been waiting days for your call! I went to the Hotel Carmen just as you told me to do. I waited and waited. How did you know I was here? Is Rafael with you? Come up to the room."

"I can't. Someone might be watching." Maria's voice was muffled. "Julie, please... Meet me down here. I've got to see you."

"But..." Juliana hesitated for a fraction of a second. "All right," she said. "Yes, all right. Stay where you are. I'll be right down."

"Hurry, Julie. Please."

Juliana was trembling when she put the phone down. Brian had told her not to leave the room but she had to see Maria. She'd talk to her, persuade her to come back here and wait for Brian. She pulled the nightgown over her head and threw it on a chair.

Quickly she dressed in a short white skirt, a T-shirt and sandals, and grabbing her purse, ran out of the room.

Maria stood just beyond the window of the tobacco shop. Her face was pale, her green eyes large with fear. She ran to Juliana and clasping her hands and said, "Quick, the car is just around the corner."

"The car? Where are we going?"

Maria tugged at her arm. "Hurry, Julie. We've got to get away before somebody sees me."

"No, wait," Juliana said, even as she allowed Maria to pull her around the corner. "Look, I'm with a man who worked with Tim. He had to leave but he'll be back in a little while. We have to wait for him; he'll know what to do."

"We can't wait!" Maria's voice was desperate. "Come on!"

The car was a late fifties model Volkswagen Bug. Maria got in and turned on the ignition.

"I've got to tell Brian!" Juliana protested as Maria jerked the car into gear and sped down the street toward the edge of town. "Maria, please, wait a minute! I can't leave like this. I've got to go back."

But Maria didn't stop. "Tell me about him, the man you said you were with," she said.

"His name is Brian McNeely. He worked with Tim, he was his friend."

"Now he's your . . . friend?"

"Yes." Juliana put her hand on Maria's arm. "We've go to go back. Brian's a capable man, he'll know what to do."

"A capable *government* man who came here to stop the rebels?" Maria shot a glance at Juliana. "That's it, isn't it, Julie? Your government sent him here to rout out the rebels, didn't they?"

"No! They sent him after me."

"After you?" The car swerved to the right toward the cane fields as Maria looked at her. "Why would the government care what you do?"

"They only cared because of my association with Emilio. They thought I came to San Benito after him—that I'd lead them to him."

"And that's exactly what you're trying to do, isn't it?" Maria's voice was bitter.

Juliana stared at her sister-in-law. What was the matter with Maria? What was she talking about? Before she could speak Maria said, "Emilio loves you, Julie. You shouldn't have run away from him when you were at the Quinta. You say this Brian McNeely is your friend, but I suspect he's much more than that. You no longer care what happens to Emilio, to any of us."

"Of course I care," Juliana protested. "That's why I'm here. I came to San Benito because of you and Rafael. I love you both, I want to help you."

"Do you?"

"Of course I do!" Juliana looked at her sister-in-law in surprise, not understanding the animosity she heard in Maria's voice. "We've got to talk," she said. "Pull over."

Maria hesitated, then slowed the car and pulled over to the side of the road.

"Okay." Juliana took a deep breath. "Now suppose you tell me what this is all about, why you're so angry with me."

"I'm not angry with you, but you don't understand about my country." Maria looked at Juliana and with a sigh said, "This goes back a long time, long before I met Tim. To make you understand I have to tell you a little about San Benito." She took a package of cigarettes out of her purse, pulled one out and lit it.

"I thought you quit smoking a year ago," Juliana said.

"I did." María drew smoke into her lungs and leaned back against the seat. "San Benito is a small country," she said, "much smaller than your Rhode Island. It lies close to Brazil but because we were conquered by Spain in 1525 our language is Spanish rather than Portuguese. Our people are mestizos, a mixture of Indian and Spanish blood. For the past sixty years we've been ruled by a dictatorship."

Maria smashed her cigarette out in the ashtray. "For more than forty years Renaldo Sanchez-Fuentes ruled us. Now it is his son, Alberto. We have almost no schools and only one hospital. Babies die of malnutrition. People disappear or are thrown into prison for no reason." She looked at Juliana. "There is a time when people must fight to live as free men and women. That time is now, Julie. We can't continue to live—to allow our children to live—with this kind of oppression any longer."

Juliana scowled in concentration. "You say 'we,' Maria. I understand that these are your people, but this isn't your country, not anymore. It isn't your fight. It—"

"Of course it's my fight!" Maria said angrily. "I can't turn my back on my family, on my country. I believe in what we're fighting for."

"Yes, so do I," Juliana said, "if what you say is true."

"Then why are you trying to stop us?"

"Stop you?" Juliana stared at Maria in surprise. "What are you talking about?"

"You and your government man, your Brian McNeely. He came here to try to stop the revolution."

"I've already told you, Brian doesn't have anything to do with this. He came to San Benito to find me because he thought I'd lead him to Emilio."

"But don't you see, it's the same thing!" Maria's voice rose. "Emilio will *be* the new government. He's our leader. He's the one people follow." She turned on Juliana and in a furious voice said, "Your Mr. McNeely wants to take him back to the United States. We must prevent that at any cost." She started the car and eased it back onto the road.

Juliana stared at her sister-in-law. Was that why Maria had telephoned her? Was that why she was in the car now, heading for God only knew where? Was she the bait for Brian to come after her? The thought, the certainty of it chilled Juliana. Maria had tricked her into coming with her so they could get their hands on Brian.

As furious as she was frightened, Juliana made herself speak calmly. "Did you know that Tim had been investigating the rebel movement here in San Benito when he was killed?" she asked.

"No! That's impossible."

"But it's true. Maria, how can you support these people if there's even the remotest possibility that they were responsible for Tim's death?"

Maria's face paled. "You don't know what you're saying!" she protested. "They wouldn't have... They know what Tim meant to me. You're trying to confuse me."

"Tim never spoke to you about San Benito? He never asked you questions?"

"Yes, but..." A look of uncertainty crossed Maria's face. "But that doesn't mean he was involved in trying to put down the rebel movement here."

"Doesn't it?" Juliana leaned her head back against the seat. "Where are we going?" she asked.

"To the mountains." Maria didn't look at Juliana; she kept her eyes on the road ahead.

Juliana stiffened with fear. "Is Emilio there?"

"They're all there."

For a moment Juliana didn't speak. Then she took a deep breath and said, "You're one of them, aren't you?" And knew without being told that Maria Espinosa, her brother's widow, was a part of the plot to overthrow the government of San Benito.

She thought then of Brian and knew that he would come after her. He'd go to the Quinta and if she wasn't there he'd look for her in the mountains. They'd be waiting for him, for it was Brian they wanted, not her.

Juliana closed her eyes. Brian, she thought, what have I done?

Chapter 8

The blood-red ruby in the simple gold setting sparkled from the shop window. Brian paused. A smile crossed his rugged features and without stopping to think about it he opened the door and went inside. Ten minutes later he came out, the small blue box with the ruby ring snug in his pocket.

He knew that Julie was upset about leaving San Benito. He couldn't do anything about that, but he could ease her going with the promise of what was to come—an official engagement and a wedding as soon as he returned to Miami.

Brian had mentioned the word *marriage* to Juliana and each time he had seen a fleeting look of doubt cross her face, probably because they were so different. He was pretty sure Julie thought of him as government-issue establishment, the establishment she'd rebelled against since her college days. But in spite of their differences, whether real or imagined, Julie couldn't deny what was between them.

He hadn't said the words, "Will you marry me?" but he would today, and he knew she would say yes. His chest swelled with the certainty of Julie's love, and of his love for her. He wouldn't fool himself into thinking that they'd have a smooth-as-silk marriage because he was every bit as stubborn and as set in his ways as Julie. While he was out trying to uphold the law she'd be out breaking it—if she thought the law was wrong.

Brian grinned to himself as he drew near the docks. She'd be a rambunctious handful and he doubted if he'd ever tame her, but what joy there'd be in trying! He thought of all the days and nights ahead, of holding her, loving her, and felt his body filling with desire. He'd never felt about another woman what he felt for Julie, with Julie. He wanted to spend the rest of his life with her.

When Brian reached the docks he asked about the passenger ferry from Belém.

"Something is wrong with it, *señor*," the owner of a small skiff told him. "It will be out of service until the end of the week."

"Is there any other kind of boat that will take passengers to Belém?"

The man shook his head. "I'm not sure, *señor*. Occasionally the mail boat will take passengers."

Brian thanked him, then hurried down the dock to find the skipper of the mail boat.

"I leave every morning at five-thirty," the skipper told him. "I don't like to take passengers unless it's an emergency."

"It's an emergency," Brian said. "My wife has to go to Belém to catch a plane for Miami."

The man scratched his chin, frowned, then said, "It will cost you one hundred dollars, *señor*."

Brian nodded. "I'll give it to you in the morning before you leave."

"Have her here at five-fifteen. I won't wait if she's late."

"She'll be here." Brian shook hands with the man, then turned away and hurried back down the dock, anxious to get back to Julie. They'd make the most of tonight, he told himself. They'd go to their seaside restaurant. He'd feed her lobster and caress the warm silkiness of her leg under the table. After dinner they'd dance again because he loved holding her as they moved to the music. He loved the slow rise of passion when their bodies touched, the holding back while the heat built between them. He'd look at her face through the veil of smoke as they danced. It would be as it had been; her eyes would grow heavy with desire, her lips would part as though waiting for his kiss.

Tonight. Tonight when the waiting became a sweet torture he would kiss every inch of Julie's lovely body so that when they were parted he might remember every line and curve of her, every warm and secret place. The memory of her would be imprinted in his heart and in his mind until they were together again. He would make love to her fiercely and completely, shattering her with his love so that she would remember, so that he would be forever a part of her, as she would always be a part of him.

Brian closed his hand around the ring box. He'd give it to her tonight at dinner, slip it on her finger and say, "I love you, Julie. Will you marry me?"

When Brian reached the hotel he ran up the stairs to the room and knocked on the door. There was no answer. He knocked again. "Julie?" he called. "Come on, Julie, open the door."

When there was no answer Brian stood back and glowered. Then he shook his head and grinned. So she was still mad. Well, she'd get over it. He wouldn't wait until tonight to give her the ring, but give it to her now. And afterward they'd make love and everything would be all right.

Brian went back downstairs. "My wife is in the shower," he told the desk clerk. "She didn't answer my knock. May I have another key, please?"

He put the key in the lock and opened the door. "Julie?" he called. She didn't answer. The bathroom door was open. The bathroom was empty. He went out to the balcony. She wasn't there. He stood in the middle of the room, then he went out on the balcony again. As he looked out at the sea he put his hand in his pocket and felt the ring box.

Brian felt hollow inside, then angry. But fear was mixed with his anger because he was afraid that Julie had rushed headlong into a situation far more dangerous than she imagined. She'd run away from him because of Maria and Rafael, he told himself. Because of her concern for their safety. He forced himself to remember that her leaving had nothing to do with Emilio.

Brian sat down on the bed. The white nightgown that Julie had thrown aside lay at the foot. He picked it up and held it to his face. The material was soft. The faint scent of her perfume clung to it. He closed his eyes and breathed in the scent. The thought of what had passed between them last night, of her sweet wildness, her surrender and her fine passion, and the thought that she had left him made him groan aloud. He closed his eyes. What if she hadn't left him to go to Maria and the boy? What if she *had* gone to Emilio?

A look of pain crossed Brian's face. Then his expression hardened. He was a professional with a job to do, and by God he'd do it. Getting up he grabbed his suitcase, opened it, and slid back a special panel in the bottom. He took out a shoulder holster, strapped it on, then took out a short-barreled revolver and shoved it in the holster. With a last, bitter look around the room, he went downstairs and arranged for a rental car.

The little Volkswagen coughed and sputtered as it climbed higher into the mountains. Thirty minutes ago Maria had turned off the main road onto a rutted dirt path that was overgrown on both sides with ditch weeds. They were on a narrow one-lane road that seemed to go straight up. On one side the mountain

rose to the volcano of Manitura, on the other side it
dropped to four thousand feet.

The two women had not spoken for over an hour.
It didn't seem possible to Juliana that this was Tim's
wife, a woman she thought she knew. This dark-
haired, green-eyed woman was a stranger, a woman
from a different country, a different culture. Juliana
wanted to reach out to her. She wanted to tell her that
her home was now in Miami. She looked at Maria, at
the pale, set face, and said nothing.

Sun beat on the roof of the small car. The air that
came in through the open windows was hot, humid
and heavy with the smell of jungle dampness. Maria
smoked incessantly, fumbling in the package beside
her, shaking out cigarette after cigarette, drawing the
smoke into her lungs until Juliana wanted to snatch
the pack away and throw it out of the window. When
she could stand the silence no longer she said, "How
much farther?"

"We're almost there." Maria slowed to a snail's
pace. Then suddenly, as they rounded a curve, they
saw a man dressed in a camouflage uniform standing
in the middle of the road, legs spread, holding a rifle
in the crook of his arm.

Maria stopped. "Don't speak," she said to Juliana
as she stepped from the car. She waved to the man.
"Hola, Pablo. ¿Qué pasa?"

"The woman is with you?"

"Of course. Stand aside and let us pass."

He shouldered the rifle and motioned them on.
When the car drew abreast of him he peered in the

window at Juliana and whistled. *"Muy bonita,"* he said with a wink. "Emilio is a lucky man."

Juliana glanced at Maria. She knew now that Emilio had sent Maria for her. Emilio and Ricardo Zamora.

Other men and a few women appeared at the side of the road, dressed in similar camouflage uniforms. The road gave way to a jungle path and Juliana saw tents among the trees. Maria pulled the Volkswagen off the path and parked it. She pointed to their right and said, "There's the cabin. Come on."

Juliana got out of the car. A couple of men and a woman stepped closer, eyeing her curiously. The men were bearded and their hair was shaggy. She was uneasy among them. She walked stiffly with her back straight and chin up, clutching her purse with nervous fingers.

The cabin, the size of an average eight-room house, stood on the slope of the mountain. A wooden porch ran the length of it. The sides were made of logs, the roof of palm fronds. As Juliana looked up at it, Emilio stepped out on the porch. He raised his hand but before he could speak a small figure darted around him.

"Julie!" Rafael cried. *"Tía* Julie!" He raced down the steps of the porch and she dropped to her knees as he launched himself at her.

"Rafael!" She hugged him to her. "Oh, Rafa, I'm so glad to see you."

"Where you been, *Tía* Julie? I lost a tooth. See? Here in front. I wiggled it and wiggled it and it just fell out and I didn't cry.'' He tugged at her hand. "Can we go back home now that you're here, Julie?" His brown eyes were suddenly solemn. He dropped his voice to a whisper. "I don't like this place," he said close to her ear. "There's nowhere to play and nobody to play with."

"That's too bad, honey." Juliana ruffled his soft brown hair. "We'll talk to your mom and see what she says." She stood up and, taking his hand, faced Maria and said, "He shouldn't be here in this...this jungle."

"San Benito is his home." Maria's voice was defensive. "It's where he belongs."

"Rafa's an American. He belongs in his own country. He..." Juliana stopped as Emilio came toward her. Tightening her hand on Rafael's she said, "Hello, Emilio."

"Hello, Julie." He kissed her cheek. "Welcome to our jungle paradise."

"Your paradise is a rebel camp," she said. "When does the revolution start?"

"Soon." A muscle in Emilio's cheek jumped. "Please come inside." He glanced at Maria. "Take Rafael to his room and stay there with him. I want to speak to Julie alone."

Maria nodded. She glanced quickly at Juliana, then away. "Come along, Rafa," she said to her son.

"But I want to stay with *Tía* Julie." The little boy's lower lip came out in a pout.

"You'll see her later." Before the boy could answer Maria picked him up and hurried into the house with him.

Emilio took Juliana's arm. "I know all this seems strange to you," he said. "There are things you don't understand, but I'll try to explain them to you. You're right, this is a rebel camp, and there are dozens more just like it scattered throughout the island. When the time is right we'll attack, and with God's help we'll overthrow the government of Sanchez-Fuentes."

"With God's help?" Juliana's voice was bitter. "Why do men who make war with other men always feel that God is on their side? These people are revolutionaries—you're a revolutionary." She looked at him. "That's why you were in Miami, wasn't it? You were getting arms for this war of yours. And Tim . . ." She had to steel herself to go on, to say the terrible words that had to be said. "Tim found out about it, didn't he? He got in your way and your people killed him. You used Maria, and you used me to get to him. You were responsible for my brother's death, Emilio."

His face paled. "No." He choked out the word. "I swear to you, Julie, I had nothing to do with Tim's death. It was a mistake, a—"

"A mistake!" Juliana's eyes went wide with shock. She backed away from Emilio, hands held up in front of her as though to keep him away. "My brother's death was a *mistake*?" She turned and ran blindly toward the trees. A man, big and broad, with a thatch of whiskers and a long drooping mustache, stepped in front of her and when she tried to push him aside he picked her up and swung her off her feet.

"Where are you going, little *gringa*?" He laughed. "If you want to go into the jungle then I will go with you to protect you from the beasts there. But not from me, eh? Not from Juan Garcia. I—"

"Put her down," Emilio snapped.

"Sure, boss." The big man set her on her feet. "The *gringa* is your lady?"

"Yes, she's my lady." Emilio took Juliana's hand. "I want you to tell the others that. She's never to leave the compound, but she's not to be harmed. Is that clear?"

"Sure, boss, whatever you say." Garcia bowed and with a wink said, "I am now appointing myself her personal bodyguard."

Emilio nodded. To Juliana he said, "Come along."

She looked from Emilio to Garcia. So she was a prisoner. But why? Was it because of the book Emilio had given her, or had she indeed been brought here as bait for Brian? She was sure they thought if they had her Brian would coming looking for her. And when they caught him? A chill of fear ran through Juliana's body.

Inside the cabin there was a living room with a big stone fireplace, a sofa, several rockers, and a long table. An Indian rug covered the wooden floor and there was a gun rack on one wall.

"Would you like a glass of wine?" Emilio asked.

Juliana shook her head. "Skip the civilities, Emilio. I came here because Maria asked me to, because I thought she and Rafael needed me." She walked over to the fireplace and stood in front of it. "I thought that Maria and I were friends. It's hard to believe that she tricked me into coming here."

"Don't think too harshly of Maria. Our family has been trying to overthrow the Sanchez-Fuentes administration for almost fifty years. She had no choice when her father ordered her home to San Benito or when we asked her to bring you here." Emilio motioned Juliana to the sofa, and when she was seated he said, "We'll try to make you as comfortable as possible during your stay with us. I don't want to lock you in a room, and I won't if you'll you give me your word you won't try to run away again."

"I won't give you my word." Juliana lifted her chin. "I'll escape the very first chance I get."

"Julie . . ." Emilio put his hand on her arm but she shrugged it away. "Then I'll have to lock you up. I don't want to but you leave me no choice."

Emilio sat next to her on the sofa. "I don't want any harm to come to you, Julie. You mean a great deal to me, you must know that."

"I know that your revolution killed my brother. I know that you used me."

"I didn't use you, Julie. The way I feel about you has nothing to do with ideologies or revolutions." Emilio took her hand in his. "You're important to me, Julie. I love you."

"Don't . . . don't say that, Emilio. I don't want to hear it."

"But it's true, Julie. I do love you. I'm so sorry about Tim. I—" He stopped as a door opened and Ricardo Zamora came into the room.

"I see our guest has arrived." Zamora came quickly across the room and smiled down at Julie. "*Bienvenida*, welcome to our camp. I hope you won't try to escape from here the way you did at the Quinta. I'm afraid you'd find the mountains a much more dangerous place."

Juliana stood up and faced him. "I want to know why I'm here," she said coldly. "I'm an American citizen. You have no right to keep me a prisoner."

"A prisoner? My dear Miss Thornton, you're not a prisoner, you're our guest."

She glared at him. Hands on her hips she took a step forward. "Your guest wants to leave," she snapped.

Zamora fingered his trim white mustache and with a smile said, "I'm afraid that's not possible. A lack of transportation, you see."

"I see. Okay, Zamora, what do you want with me? Is it the book Emilio gave me? Because if it is, I haven't got it with me. It's back in Miami."

"It isn't the book we want, Miss Thornton, at least not in this moment. We're interested in something... in someone who is already here in San Benito. Someone whom, I'm afraid, will give us a great deal of trouble if he isn't stopped."

"Someone?" Julie took a step backward. "I don't know what you mean."

"Don't play games with me, Miss Thornton. You know very well I'm talking about Mr. McNeely." Zamora smiled at her. "We want to . . . have a chat with him. And what better way to get him here than to have him come after you?"

So it was Brian they wanted. They'd killed Tim, now they wanted Brian, and they were using her to get him.

Well, they wouldn't get him! She'd made a huge mistake when she allowed Maria to bring her here, but she wouldn't make another one. She'd do whatever she had to do to prevent Brian from falling into their trap.

Juliana looked at Emilio. He'd told her he cared about her and she believed him. But the revolution was equally important to him—perhaps more so. He wouldn't let anything or anyone stand in the way of its success.

She had to get away from the camp. She had to find Brian and warn him before it was too late.

Chapter 9

Zamora held her chair out. "Please," he said, with an attempt at gallantry, "sit next to me."

Juliana's nod was brief, her face set and angry. She knew, as everyone at the table knew, that she was a prisoner. The room they'd locked her in earlier wasn't a cell with bars on the windows, but there was a lock on the door and a guard posted on the porch outside the open screenless window. What hurt and angered her the most was that she'd been brought to this mountain hideaway, that she had been *betrayed* by a woman she thought of as a friend as well as a sister-in-law.

But the hurt and anger weren't as important as the fact that Brian's life was in danger because of her. If anything happened to him it would be her fault. She had to escape, had to warn Brian to stay away from this place.

Juliana clasped her hands together under the table. What had he thought when he returned from the docks? Did he think that she'd purposely run away from him? Or that she'd been taken by force? She looked at the food in front of her and shuddered when she realized how frantic he must be, how angry. She should have left him a note telling him that Maria had phoned, but she'd expected to take Maria back to their room. If she'd known she was coming here . . . if . . .

Juliana looked across the table and saw Maria watching her. Doubt and shame were in Maria's green eyes, and something else, a plea for understanding. But Juliana was too angry to be understanding. She'd left Brian without an explanation and she would draw him into a trap because he cared for her. His life was in danger because of Maria. She looked at Maria coldly and without expression, and turned her attention to Rafael.

The little boy sat beside his mother, silent, head bowed, scarcely touching his food.

"You must eat, Rafa," Maria said softly.

"I don't like this," he mumbled. "I want a hamburger."

"He's been in the United States too long," Otero said loudly. "Hamburgers, hotdogs, and big cars—trappings of a decadent society." He leaned across the table and pointed his finger at Rafael. "Eat what is on your plate. If you don't, I myself will administer a thrashing you'll never forget."

"Please, Miguel." Maria sounded frightened. "Rafa's only a little boy. He—"

"A spoiled little boy." He jabbed a finger against Rafael's chest. "Eat!" he ordered.

Rafael lifted his small hand. Without looking at Miguel Otero he picked up his fork, placed it across his plate, and pushed his plate into the middle of the table.

With a muttered oath Otero cuffed Rafael on the side of his head, shoved the plate back in front of him, and fastening his fingers in Rafael's hair forced the boy's head toward his plate.

Rafael cried out in pain. Tears gathered in his eyes as he tried to squirm away.

Suddenly, before anyone could move, Juliana jumped to her feet. She grabbed a handful of Otero's hair with one hand, and in her other hand grasped her fork like a weapon, ready to strike.

"Let him go." The words were spoken slowly, clearly. Her eyes were hot coals of fire.

Otero loosened his hand. Juliana released her grip on his hair, but she held the fork poised and ready. Otero glared at her. His small black eyes were narrowed, his nostrils pinched white with outrage. He drew his hand back but before he could strike Juliana, Emilio hit him across the face.

"Don't touch her." Emilio's voice was flat, deadly. "Don't you ever touch her or Rafael again."

For a moment the two men glared at each other. Then Otero looked away. Without a word he stalked out of the room.

No one spoke, then Zamora said, "You shouldn't have done that, Señorita Thornton. Miguel is a hot-headed man. He won't forget that you have embarrassed him in front of us. Rafael is his nephew; he feels that he has the right, because Rafael's father is dead, to act as his parent. All boys need a strong hand." His dark eyes were intent as they stared into Juliana's. "You must understand that San Benito is Rafael's home now. He has to learn to adapt to our way of life. In a few years he'll be old enough to fight for his country. He won't be able to if he is coddled by women."

"He's five years old." Juliana's face was tense with anger. "And San Benito isn't his home, Señor Zamora. He's a citizen of the United States. That's his home; that's were he belongs."

A muscle twitched in Zamora's jaw. He spoke coldly. "You're here as our guest, Señorita Thornton. You'll be well treated as long as you don't try to interfere." He motioned to her chair. "Now please, sit down. Let us continue our meal."

They ate in silence. Rafael picked at his food and when he had finished he came to Juliana to tell her good-night. He put his arms around her neck and buried his face against her shoulder. She held him in her arms and silently she vowed that someway, somehow, she would get Rafael away from here.

"Thank you for what you did," Maria said as she took Rafael's hand. She leaned close, her voice dropped to a whisper. "Forgive me, Julie. Try…please try to understand."

But Juliana didn't answer. She touched Rafael's cheek and did not look at his mother.

Juliana waited a long time, there in the darkness of her room, timing the pacing of the guard outside her window until she knew his moves by heart. Up and down the porch. Forty paces up, forty paces back. Every eight or ten minutes he paused near one of the wooden posts to light a cigarette. By two-fifteen Juliana was poised and ready when he turned his back and started to the far end of the porch.

As quietly as a cat, she slid out of the window onto the porch and flattened herself behind one of the posts. She scarcely dared to breathe when the guard started back toward her. He hesitated only a few steps away, turned, and as he walked away she slid off the porch and began to crawl past the bushes toward the trees.

The night was still. Suddenly Juliana remembered the large man, Juan Garcia, who had stopped her earlier today. She felt a chill of fear, then shrugged it off. This wasn't the time for nerves. She had to get away. She had to find Brian.

The jungle closed in around Juliana, dark and forbidding, smelling of dampness and tree rot. A parrot screeched in one of the trees above her head and she jumped with fright. Take it easy, she told herself. You've made it this far. Just keep going. Just... A tree loomed in front of her. Hanging moss brushed her face and suddenly it was as though she were a child again, back among the old oak trees hung heavy with

Spanish moss. She remembered how frightened she'd been, how her fear had been an almost living, breathing thing that seemed to close in around her as she'd plunged through the trees with the feel of the moss brushing against her body.

For a moment Juliana stopped. She told herself that she wasn't a child, that her fear of the night and of the jungle, of the things that dwelt there, wasn't important. She had to get to Brian. She had—

Somewhere behind her a twig snapped. She stopped. The breath caught in her throat. Her heart felt as though it would burst against her ribs. She waited a moment, then took a cautious step forward. It's only an animal, she told herself. A *small* animal. She turned around, trying to see through the darkness, through the shadows of ghostly moss-hung trees. Her palms were damp and she felt the pulse beating in her throat. Carefully she shuffled one foot, thinking if there was an animal behind her she would scare it away. There was no sound. She released a breath and started forward. Go on, she told herself. Just go on.

Juliana took two steps before another twig snapped, closer this time. She hesitated only a moment, then thoroughly frightened, plunged ahead into the darkness. Footsteps thudded behind her and she knew it wasn't an animal. It was—

A hand grabbed Juliana's shoulder and spun her around. Through the darkness she saw a face. Miguel Otero! She screamed once before he slapped a hand over her mouth. "You do that again, *gringa*, I hurt you real bad," he threatened.

For a split second Juliana was too terrified to move, then she struck out—a blow with the back of her fist across his face, a knee to his groin. Otero hissed with pain and let her go. But before she could spin away he grabbed her again. He hooked a foot behind her foot and shoved her to the ground. She rolled away from him, skittering on hands and knees on the damp jungle floor as she tried to get away. Otero grabbed an ankle and hauled her back. She screamed again, screamed until a hand slashed across her face, stunning her, frightening her to silence.

Otero straddled Juliana. He put his face close to hers. He fastened a hand in her hair and yanked her closer. His hand tightened in her hair, and he tugged until tears came to her eyes. "How does it feel, *gringa*? You did it to me, now it's your turn. But you're lucky, there is no one to see your shame." He pressed his legs closer to her body, squeezing her, holding her. "You come here to San Benito with your high and mighty ways. You think you're too good for us, you scoff at our revolution, you try to betray us to your government."

"I don't give a damn about your revolution." Juliana tried to pull away, but he kept her pinned to the ground with his body. "I came here because of Maria and Rafael," she said. "I—"

"Liar!" Otero cuffed her on the side of the head. "You came here for your government. I know it and Zamora knows it. But that poor bastard Emilio is too crazy in love with you to see who you really are. Now you try to escape so you can bring the other agent into our camp." He grabbed Juliana's chin and forced her to look at him. "But if Emilio is blind, I'm not. I'll wait for McNeely and I'll kill him." His fingers bit into her skin. "But killing is not what I have planned for you, *gringa.*"

Small black eyes, gleaming like a night-stalking jungle animal stared down at Juliana. He put his hand on the top of her shirt and ripped it open. As he did so she heaved her body up against his. With every ounce of her strength she bucked hard, smacked the edge of her hand against his throat, and rolled away from him.

Otero gasped for air. Then with a muttered oath he came after Juliana. She screamed when he grabbed her belt, kicked out and connected with his shoulder, then was pulled, face down toward him, clawing and scratching in the earth as she struggled to break free of his grasp. He was breathing hard when he turned her over. "Now," he muttered. "Now, *gringa.*"

A figure loomed up out of the darkness. A fist lashed out and caught Otero on the head. He cried out once. The fist lashed out again and he toppled, unconscious, over Juliana.

"*¡Cabrón!*" Juan Garcia spat as he kicked Otero aside. He leaned over Juliana and helping her to her feet asked, "Are you all right? Did he hurt you?"

Her legs wobbled and she had to grasp Garcia's arm to keep from falling. "No," she managed to say. "I'm all right."

"You'd better be. If you aren't I'll kill that son of a female turkey." He pulled a gun from his holster and for a moment Juliana thought he meant to shoot

Otero. Instead he fired in the air, then yelled, "I've found her. She's over here."

There was an answering shout. Then, before Juliana could control her trembling, Emilio burst through the trees.

"Julie!" he cried. "My God, Julie, are you all right?" He ran to her, grasping her arms to make sure she was all right. Then he looked down and saw Miguel Otero. "What happened?" he said. "What?—"

"This rotten *cabrón* attacked her," Garcia said.

Emilio looked at Juliana. "My God," he said, and with a cry pulled her into his arms.

"She's all right," Garcia said. "A little shook up, but I got here before he did her any real harm." He kicked the semiconscious man and was rewarded with a groan. "Something ought to be done about this poor excuse for a human being though." He kicked Otero again. "What do you want done with him?"

"Lock him up in one of the outbuildings." Emilio's voice was hard. "If he gives you any trouble shoot him." He looked down at Julie. "Come along, *querida*," he said. "I'll take you back to the camp."

Juliana didn't speak. No matter how she felt about Emilio, he was a comforting presence, someone familiar, someone she knew wouldn't harm her. His arm felt good and strong around her waist as she leaned against him and let him guide her through the jungle. For the moment at least she could forget that he was her enemy and she his prisoner.

When they got back to the cabin Zamora and Alejandro Espinosa were on the porch with the guard. But before they could speak Emilio said, "I'm going to take Juliana to her room. She's had enough for one night." He led her past them, into the cabin and down the hall to her room. When he closed the door he said, "You shouldn't have tried to escape, Julie. Are you sure you're all right?"

"Yes, Emilio, I'm . . . I'm all right." She shivered. "But if Garcia hadn't come along when he did, if he hadn't found me..." She clasped her arms tight to her body. Her voice shook so badly she couldn't go on.

"I should have let Garcia kill him," Emilio muttered. He took Juliana's hand and led her to the bed. "I'm so sorry that you're involved in this, Julie. Please believe me, darling, I didn't want it to work out this way."

"You sent Maria for me," she said accusingly. "You trapped me into coming here."

"Only to protect you, Julie, so you'd be where I know you're safe." He sat down beside her. "Things are happening fast. In another few months we'll be ready to fight, but there's trouble. Zamora's trying to wrest control away from me and he's using you to do it. He's told the others you're dangerous, that you're working with McNeely, spying on us for your government." Emilio ran a tired hand across his face. "But it's McNeely he really wants, Julie, not you."

Emilio put an arm around her shoulders. "I was afraid that if you were with McNeely he'd kill you, too. I couldn't let that happen, darling. I wanted you here where I could protect you." He put a finger under her chin and lifted her face to his. "I care about you, Julie. Leaving you in Miami was the hardest thing I've ever done.''

Zamora wanted Brian dead! Juliana looked at Emilio. She tried to gather her thoughts, tried to think clearly. Emilio loved her. He wasn't a murderer, he was a decent man. Stalling for time she said, ''You weren't involved in Tim's death, were you?''

Emilio took her hands in his. ''On the grave of my parents I swear that I was not.'' He brought her hands to his lips and kissed them. ''But I *am* a revolutionary, Julie. I've smuggled arms from your country into San Benito and I've fought against men here who would stop the revolution. I'll fight for freedom in San Benito as long as there is breath in my body. I'll kill if I have to.''

''What about Brian McNeely?'' Juliana asked softly. ''Will you stand by and let Zamora kill him?''

She felt a sigh run through Emilio's body. ''I'll stop him if I can. But if McNeely gets in the way, then I'll do what has to be done.'' He stood up. For a moment neither of them spoke, then Emilio said, ''Are you in love with him, Julie?''

Juliana raised her eyes and looked at him. From somewhere deep inside herself she found the strength to lie, to say, ''I thought I was, but I . . . I was so lost, Emilio. You'd left me. I came to San Benito to try to find you, to find Maria and Rafael. I was so alone. Brian found me and I was as much his prisoner as I am yours now.''

Emilio drew her into his arms. ''My poor Julie,'' he said as he kissed her brow. ''You must rest now, dear.

We'll talk about this in the morning." At the door he stopped. "I'm not a murderer," he said. "But I love my country. I'll do whatever I have to to lead her to freedom."

He left Juliana alone then. She hadn't cried before, but now hot tears flooded her eyes and streaked her cheeks. She turned her face into the pillow and cried for Brian because she loved him, and for Emilio because she couldn't love him and had lied to him. When she had cried all of her tears she lay looking up at the ceiling while a myriad of thoughts ran round and round in her brain. She had lied and she would again. She'd do anything that was necessary to protect Brian. For he was her love; he was her life.

Brian held the steering wheel tightly as he pushed the small car faster and faster. His face was strained and pale, his eyes so dark and angry that they looked as though they'd been chipped from mountain rock. There was no softness in him now, no hint of the man who had touched Juliana with tender hands. This was a coldly professional man with a job to do. Any remembrance of love, of tenderness or compassion, had been thrust to the back of his brain.

But thoughts of Juliana, of her softness and the way she had felt in his arms, kept finding their way into his mind. Okay, he told himself, so you fell for her. You love her—no, loved her—and maybe that proves you're human. Maybe she loved you, for a while, but don't let it go to your head because it sure as hell didn't last long. Brian set his jaw. It only lasted until Emilio arrived on the scene—until his own back was turned. Then she'd left him, without a word, without even a note.

Brian thought about the ruby he'd left back in the hotel room. God, what a fool he'd been! He'd actually believed that Julie had loved him enough to marry him. He struck the steering wheel and cursed aloud. She was a rebel, a fighter for lost causes. Save the whale, no more nukes, fight oppression. Brian ran a hand across his chin. Was that how Emilio got to her? Was the San Benito revolution another cause for her? Had she decided to fight beside Emilio?

He had to get her away from Emilio and from San Benito before she ruined her life. It didn't matter that whatever there'd been between them no longer existed. Tim had been his friend. He'd promised Jack Kelly that he would bring Julie back and he would—after he'd taken care of Emilio Martinez.

Thirty minutes later Brian turned off the road and headed toward the Quinta Espinosa. A hundred yards from the house he pulled the car off to the side behind a clump of trees. Then, bent low, revolver in his hand, he went slowly and carefully toward the house.

He was almost there when he spotted the guard Julie had told him about. The man looked tough and mean and the rifle in his arm deadly. Brian dropped to the ground, waited, then using his elbows, edged slowly forward. Five feet away, Brian sprang to his feet, and with a cry that sent a covey of birds flying high off the ground, leaped upon the guard.

With a startled cry the man tried to jump back. But it was too late. Brian was over him, and he was on the ground, flat on his back, with a pair of steel-blue eyes blazing into his.

"Where is she?" Brian demanded. "Where have they taken her?"

"I don't know what you're talking about," the guard said, struggling to break free. Brian shoved his arm hard against the man's throat. "I'm talking about the *gringa, cabrón*. Where is she?" He moved his arm again and the guard gagged. Trying to break free of Brian's grip the man sucked in his breath and said, "I tell you nothing."

Brian smiled down at his victim—a terrible, slow smile that made the man stiffen with alarm. "You'll tell me, all right," Brian said softly. "Sooner or later. So make it easy on yourself, *amigo*. If they've taken Miss Thornton to that cabin in the mountains then I want to know exactly where the cabin is and how to get there. I want to know how many guerrillas there are in the camp and where the guards are posted."

"I...I'll tell you nothing," the guard said again. But his voice was less sure now, and beads of sweat had broken out on his forehead.

"Of course you will," Brian said gently. "Of course you will, *amigo*."

Forty minutes later, with the guard securely tied to a post in the barn, Brian walked back to his car. His face was pale, but the hands that held the steering wheel were steady as he headed back to the road leading to the mountains.

Chapter 10

It was very late that night before Juliana fell into a troubled sleep. She was still asleep the next morning when a noise awakened her. Startled, she opened her eyes to see Rafael poised in the window, one leg dangling inside the room.

"Good morning." She sat up in bed and ran a hand through her tousled hair. "This is a nice surprise. Come on in, I need a hug."

With a shy grin, the little boy slid his other leg over the sill. He ran across the room and jumped up on the bed. "One of the mean old guards with a gun tried to stop me, *Tía* Julie," he said. "But Juan Garcia came and he said it was okay, that I could come see you if I wanted to."

"Gosh, I'm glad you did," Juliana said as she hugged him. "I've really missed you, Rafael."

"You're going to take me back to Miami, aren't you? Me and Mama."

"I guess..." Juliana hesitated. "I guess it depends on your mother, Rafa."

"But I don't like it here, Julie. There aren't any kids to play with and there isn't any television or school or anything." Rafael pouted childishly. Lowering his voice he leaned closer and whispered. "I don't like *Tío* Miguel. He's mean and sometimes he hits me and he says, 'It's time you acted like a grown-up man.' It scared me last night when you pulled his hair. I thought he was going to kill you or something."

"He's not going to kill me, Rafa. And he's never going to hit you again." She tousled his hair. "What do you do all day, kiddo?"

Rafael shrugged. "Nothing. Mama doesn't like me to be around the soldiers, but sometimes she lets me go with Juan. And once I went down to the beach with *Tío* Emilio. He's okay."

"Do you remember how far is it down to the beach, honey?"

"Sure. We went in the jeep." He pointed to the window. "Out that road down there and it took..." His small forehead wrinkled in concentration. "It took until it was time for lunch, *Tía* Julie."

Until it was time for lunch? She supposed that depended on how hungry Rafa had been at the time. At least she knew what direction the beach was in. She'd been unsuccessful in her attempt to escape last night, but that didn't mean she'd given up. The next time she'd try to get to the beach. She had to find Brian, to warn him that Emilio and his men were waiting for him.

Yesterday Emilio had asked her to promise she wouldn't try to escape. He'd asked for her word and she'd refused to give it. Now as Rafael began to tell her about the camp and the men and women with guns, Juliana began to formulate a plan. She'd never gone back on her word before, but terrible situations called for terrible measures. She wasn't just fighting for herself now, she was fighting for Rafael and for Brian; she'd do anything to keep them safe. If she promised him she wouldn't try to escape again, Emilio might believe her. If he believed her, if he gave her the freedom of the house and the camp, she'd have a chance to get away.

"...and this great big wild pig came running through the woods and Juan shot him," Rafael said, breaking in on her thoughts. "He shot him dead and he said I wasn't ever to go into the woods without him."

"A wild pig?" Juliana thought of last night when she'd been alone in the jungle. And of Rafael, so close to the dangers that lurked there. Before she could speak there was a knock on the door. Then the key turned and Maria came in.

"I...I was looking for Rafa," Maria said hesitantly. "Juan told me he was here with you." She looked at her son. "It's time for your breakfast, *muchacho*."

"I was talking to Julie, Mama."

"That's fine, Rafa, but your breakfast is waiting. You can see Julie later." She crossed the room and taking his hand helped him off the bed. With a gentle push she started him toward the door. "Run along. I want to talk to Julie."

His lower lip came out in the all too familiar pout. But before he could say anything, Juliana said, "We'll do something later, Rafa. Maybe you can show me around the camp." She blew a kiss and was rewarded with a smile as the little boy went out and closed the door.

"The whole camp is talking about your trying to escape last night," Maria said. "Miguel is locked up in one of the storerooms and nobody knows why." She sat down at the foot of the bed. "What happened last night, Julie?"

Juliana looked at Maria with what she hoped was an appeal for sympathy on her face. "I did try to escape last night, Maria. I hate being locked up this way." Her chin wobbled and so did her voice. "I thought you were my friend, but you tricked me into coming to San Benito, and yesterday you tricked me into coming up here to the mountains. So I tried to run away. To—"

"To go to your government man? Your CIA boy-friend?" Maria's voice was angry. "*Dios*, Julie! I expected you of all people to understand what we're fighting for. You're a rebel who's always fought against injustice. How can you want to help someone who wants to destroy us?"

"Brian doesn't want to destroy you, Maria. I've already told you that he didn't come to San Benito to stop the revolution, he came after me because he thought I'd lead him to Emilio. He just wants to question Emilio about Tim's murder." Juliana hesitated. She wanted Maria to be an ally, not an enemy, so fighting against her anger she tried to speak convincingly. "I left Brian to come with you yesterday because I care about you and Rafael. You're my family, I love you."

She reached for Maria's hand. "I wasn't running to Brian last night," she said. "I was just...running. This camp, these other men, Miguel Otero." She shuddered. "He must have seen me slip out last night. He followed me and he tried...he tried..." She took a deep breath. "He would have raped me if it hadn't been for Juan."

For a moment Maria stared at Juliana. Then she put her arms around her and said, "My poor Julie. I'm so sorry. I shouldn't have called you that day in Miami. I didn't want to but they insisted that it was necessary, that you knew too much about us."

"Knew too much about you? I don't know what you're talking about."

"Zamora was afraid Emilio had jeopardized the security of the group by falling in love with you. He went crazy when he found out Emilio had given you the book of Spanish poetry."

"But I didn't read it, Maria. I put it aside until I had more time." Juliana stared at Maria. "Is that why you tricked me into coming to San Benito? To find out how much I knew? Or if I'd told anyone?''

Maria nodded. ''Zamora demanded that Emilio bring you here to prove his loyalty. He said if he didn't they'd have you...taken care of in Miami. So...I made the phone call that brought you here to San Benito.'' Maria bowed her head. ''I can't expect you to forgive me or to understand what we're fighting for, but I hope you'll try.''

''I want to understand,'' Juliana said, ''but I don't think I do. You were Tim's wife; your loyalty was to him, not to some wild revolutionary group here in San Benito.''

''This wild revolutionary group is my country's only hope for freedom,'' Maria said defensively. ''Emilio and the others love our country, they're patriots.''

''*Your* country? Your country is the United States of America. That's where you belong, that's where Rafael should be right now.'' Juliana threw back the sheet and got out of bed. Hands on her hips, she faced her sister-in-law. ''These men you call patriots were responsible for your husband's death. My *God*, Maria, were you a part of it? Part of the plot to kill Tim?''

Maria stared at Juliana, her face pale. ''How could you...how could you even think such a thing?'' she whispered. ''I loved Tim. He was my life. If I thought that Emilio...that Zamora or Miguel or any of the others had anything to do with his death I'd kill them myself. But they had nothing to do with it, Julie. Za-

mora swore on our family Bible. It was a different
group of San Benitans. It was a mistake. A—''

A mistake. This was the second time Juliana had
heard these words. Her brother's death had been a
mistake. With a moan of pain she slumped down on
the bed and covered her face with her hands.

"Julie, please." Maria knelt beside her. "Please
believe me. I loved Tim. I'll always grieve for him. But
San Benito is my home, it's where I belong until the
fight is over. Then I'll take Rafael back to my other
home and we'll be a family again." She put her arms
around Juliana and began to cry. "Please, Julie,
please try to understand."

"All right," Juliana said, trying to control her own
tears. "Don't cry, Maria."

"I want you to understand about Tim, Julie. We
didn't know anything about each other when we married. I didn't know that he was with the government,
and he didn't know I came from a family that had
been revolutionaries for the last sixty years. If we had
known..." A smile trembled on Maria's lips. "I almost said if we had known maybe we wouldn't have
fallen in love. But nothing would have changed the
way we felt about each other, Julie. We both knew
from the day we met that we belonged together. I
loved him so much." Tears filled Maria's eyes again.
"I'd never... never have done anything to harm him.
You must believe that."

"I do, Maria. And you must believe that I love you
and Rafael, that I'd never do anything to hurt you
either."

They talked more then and in a little while things were almost as they had once been between them. Maria went back to her room for a pair of shorts and a shirt that would fit Juliana. After Juliana had bathed and dressed, Maria tapped on the locked door and together the two women went into the dining room for breakfast.

They were still at the table, lingering over coffee, when Emilio entered. "Are you all right?" he asked Juliana. "I wanted to see you earlier but I thought you might want to rest this morning. You're sure you're all right?" he asked again.

Juliana nodded. "Yes, Emilio. Thanks to you and Juan Garcia. I don't think I thanked him last night, but I will today." She took a sip of the strong black coffee. "What about Otero? Is he still locked up?"

"No, damn it."

"No?" Maria looked shocked and surprised. "After what he tried to do to Julie! He—"

"I know what he did," Emilio said angrily. "Zamora and I spent most of the night shouting at each other. I wanted Miguel punished and thrown out of San Benito, but Zamora insisted he be released this morning. There wasn't much I could do about it, Maria, at least not for the moment." Emilio lowered his voice. "Zamora and I are in a power struggle. I don't like it because our main objective now must be the revolution. Who leads it isn't important. I'd gladly turn the reins over to Zamora if I thought his patriotism was totally unselfish. But there are times when I doubt that it is. We cannot fight and win and then

find we have a man who's as bad as Sanchez-Fuentes
for our new leader.''

"But you'll be our new leader." Maria's eyes flashed
with anger. "You must be, Emilio. No one loves our
country as you do. You are honest and decent, you are
the man who must be our president."

Emilio smiled at her. "If the day ever comes that I
run for president, Maria, I hope you'll be my cam-
paign manager. In the meantime I must put up with
men like Zamora and Miguel Otero because we're all
fighting for the same thing." He looked at Juliana.
"I'll keep an eye on Miguel and so will Juan. If he ever
touches you again I'll kill him myself." He pulled out
a chair across the table from her and sat down. "I
know how difficult all of this is for you, *querida*, how
hard it must be for you to understand."

"But I do understand," Juliana said. "Or at least
I'm beginning to. I wish you'd told me about your
revolution when we were in Miami together. You know
I'm a sucker for a good cause, Emilio. I'd have helped
you if I'd known what you were fighting for." She
smiled at him. "But now I do know, Emilio, and I
want to help."

"Help?" He looked skeptical.

"Well, at least I don't want to hinder." Juliana
leaned across the table and took his hand. "Darling,
have you forgotten I'm the one who got hauled off to
jail for staging a sit-in on power company property?
Who chained herself to the entrance gate at Turkey
Point? I've always been a rebel, Emilio. If you and
Maria tell me that your people are fighting against a

bad government here in San Benito then I want to be a part of it." Juliana looked him straight in the eye. "I didn't understand when I ran away last night, and from the Quinta before. If you'd told me, Emilio, if you and Maria had explained about the revolution I would have understood."

Emilio's dark eyes softened. Thoughtfully he reached for a mug, filled it with coffee, and after he'd added sugar and stirred it, he said, "I want to believe you, Julie, but what about Brian McNeely?"

"What about him?"

"You were with him after you ran away from us at the Quinta."

"I wasn't *with* him, Emilio, I ran right into him. I told you, when I ran away from the Quinta I was afraid. Not of you, but of Zamora and the others." Juliana hesitated, knowing that if she told a partial truth she'd be more convincing. Finally she said, "Brian McNeely came to San Benito to find me because he thought I'd come here to meet you. He wanted to question you about Tim's death, Emilio. I honestly don't think he came because of the revolution."

Emilio raised the mug to his lips and took a long sip of the steaming coffee. He looked at Julie over the mug and shaking his head said, "I'm afraid you're being naive, Julie. Your government's interested in what's going on here in San Benito. I think they sent Mr. McNeely here to find out exactly what's happening and to report back." He took Juliana's hand. "If he's here because of the revolution, and not only to question me as you say, then we have to stop him. We can't allow anything or anyone to hinder us in freeing our country.'' He clasped her hand firmly. ''Julie, last night I asked you if you were in love with McNeely. You told me you weren't. Is that the truth?''

Juliana looked at him. In spite of everything that had happened she liked Emilio and didn't want to hurt him. She hated to lie but so much was at stake. Brian's life was in her hands, and she'd do anything she had to to protect him.

She made herself say, ''I'm a rebel, Emilio; Brian's the establishment that I've been fighting for a long, long time. How could I be in love with someone like him?''

''I wish I could believe you, Julie.''

''You can, Emilio.'' Oh, please believe me, she pleaded wordlessly. She took a deep breath, not liking herself, but doing what she had to do, saying the words she had to say. ''You must believe that I'd never do anything to harm you or Maria or Rafa.'' That at least was true.

A long moment passed before Emilio nodded. ''Will you give me your word that you won't try to escape again, Julie?''

The breath caught in Juliana's throat. She looked into his eyes, silently begging for forgiveness. Then she forced a smile to her lips and said, ''Of course I promise, Emilio.''

Brian waited in the jungle for night to fall. He'd parked the car back off the road and hiked six miles up into the mountains where he hid himself in the deep green foliage. He found a place close enough to the camp to see the movements there. All afternoon he watched the armed guerrillas going through practice runs, loading and reloading their rifles, running toward imaginary enemies. He saw the guards and once a large bearded man moved dangerously close to his position. As silently as a night animal Brian pulled a knife from the scabbard at his side. The man hesitated. Brian held his breath, tensed, ready. But the man moved on.

He drank water from a canteen but didn't eat. He leaned his back against a tree and thought about Julie. If they'd harmed her he'd kill them, as many of them as he could before he himself went down. Thoughts of her raced through his mind. He remembered everything about her, every sweet curve and line of her body. He thought of the first time they'd made love, of her small, involuntary cry of pain, even as she had welcomed him and drawn him closer. He thought of the way she'd looked that morning on the beach, dressed in the old-fashioned white nightgown. She'd been both sexy and prim and proper and he'd wanted her so much his teeth had ached.

Julie. Had she run away from him or had they taken her by force? He had to believe they'd taken her by force because he couldn't let himself believe that everything that had passed between them had been a lie.

It was late that afternoon before Brian saw her. She came out on the porch of the cabin with a small boy.

She was dressed in white shorts and a yellow blouse. He focused his binoculars. She looked down at the boy. He said something and she laughed. The sun glinted on her hair and Brian's breath caught. She was all right, they hadn't harmed her. The binoculars swung to the armed guard on the porch and a sense of relief flooded through his body. They hadn't hurt her, but she was a prisoner. She hadn't left him willingly. She hadn't . . . A man came out on the porch. He said something to Julie and she turned and spoke to him.

Brian drew his brows together as he focused the glasses again. The man was Emilio Martinez. He put his arm around Julie. She didn't move away. The boy ran down the steps. Emilio pulled her closer. She looked up at him and smiled.

For a moment it seemed to Brian as though a part of him died. A terrible coldness rushed through his veins. He narrowed his eyes in fury as he watched Julie and Emilio Martinez together, their arms around each other.

Brian's hand shook when he lowered the binoculars. Steady, he told himself, steady. She made a fool out of you, McNeely, but you're a professional with a job to do. You came here to get her, to take her and Martinez back to Miami, and that's what you're going to do.

He'd wait for nightfall when the camp was quiet and the rebel soldiers were asleep. He'd watch and he'd find out where Julie's room was and he'd go in after her. Then he'd go after Emilio.

Night came. Brian settled back against a tree to wait. Once he thought he heard a movement. He took his gun out. Above him in the trees a parrot screeched, an owl hooted a reply. Nerves, he told himself.

Brian didn't see the man who loomed suddenly out of the jungle until it was too late. Still, he almost made it. He had his hand on the knife when the blow came. Then the knife slid from his hand and blackness closed in around him.

Chapter 11

Dinner that night was almost pleasant. Maria had loaned Juliana a summer dress and sandals and Juliana had washed her hair and borrowed a bit of Maria's makeup and perfume. If she was going to do an adequate job of pretending to be happy about the situation she was in, or at least accepting it, she'd do it looking the very best she could.

Emilio sat next to her, Maria and Rafael across from her. Ricardo Zamora was in his usual place at the head of the table, Alejandro Espinosa on his right, Javier Gallo on his left.

Zamora was in an expansive mood. He offered Juliana extra helpings of everything, he poured her wine, he smiled at her over his wineglass and told her how lovely she looked. Juliana summoned a smile and thanked him. She knew that very likely Emilio had told him about their earlier conversation and that she had given her word not to escape. As her gaze met Zamora's, Juliana wondered whether he believed what Emilio had told him or if he was only playing a cat-and-mouse game with her.

"Women should always wear dresses, never trousers," he said. "Trousers are for men, they make women look less feminine. Femininity always brings out the best in a man, doesn't it?" He winked at Juliana. "You have poor Emilio eating out of your hand, and for that I must congratulate you." He laughed and to Emilio he said, "Be careful, my boy, lest the little *gringa* lead you down the garden path."

"Wherever Julie leads me I'll gladly follow." Emilio said, covering her hand with his.

"Well spoken." Zamora nodded his approval. "It's so touching to see that love has converted our little spitfire into a docile, loving creature. Congratulations, Emilio."

Emilio tightened his hand on Juliana's. "Julie has always been a loving creature. I'm afraid I'd find a docile woman quite dull, Ricardo. And believe me, Julie is never dull." He smiled at Juliana, then turning back to Zamora said, "She understands what we're fighting for, Ricardo. She's given me her word that she won't try to escape again."

"Her word? How nice. When our revolution is over, Emilio, I suppose you and Señorita Julie will live happily ever after, right here in San Benito. Have you told her that you expect to be our president?" For the briefest fraction of a second Zamora's eyes were ice-water cold. Then he looked at Juliana and said, "How would you like to be our First Lady, Señorita Julie? Would that please you?"

"That's a leading question, Señor Zamora. The revolution must first be won, mustn't it?"

"It will be won, *señorita*. Make no mistake about that."

Zamora turned back to his dinner and the meal was finished in silence. He didn't speak until their coffee had been served. Then he turned to Juliana and said, "I have a surprise for you. I've been saving it for dessert."

Juliana heard the barely restrained excitement, the venom in his voice, and felt a chill of foreboding run down her spine. Before she could speak Zamora turned to Alejandro and said, "Why don't you bring in our surprise?"

Alejandro grinned at Zamora as he pushed back his chair. Juliana looked at Emilio, who shrugged, then across the table at Maria. She too looked puzzled. "What's the s'prise?" Rafael asked. "Ice cream?"

"Something much more interesting than ice cream," Zamora said with a chuckle. His long, thin fingers drummed the tabletop. "Much more interesting," he repeated.

Juliana stared down at the table. She didn't know what was going on, only that Zamora was excited, that he'd planned whatever was about to happen, and that it had something to do with her. Whatever it was, she thought, she wouldn't give him the satisfaction of looking either curious or afraid. She raised her head and smiled at him, blandly, sweetly. I'm not afraid of you, she tried to tell him by her expression. Bring on your surprise, Zamora.

But the smile died on Juliana's face when the door opened. The color drained from her face and she had to grasp the edge of the table to keep from crying out.

Brian stood in the door, held up by Alejandro Espinosa and Juan Garcia. His face was bruised. There was a gash on the side of his head.

"Bring him closer," Zamora ordered. "Yes, that's it. Good evening, Señor McNeely. It's a shame you weren't able to join us for dinner. I believe you know everyone."

Brian looked at Julie. Her face was pale and still, her eyes veiled, her expression guarded. She looked very beautiful in her blue dress. Her red hair curled softly around her shoulders; he could smell her perfume.

He'd been right! She had come here—to Emilio—willingly.

Emilio put his arm protectively around her shoulders. "What in the hell's going on, Ricardo?" he demanded. "Who is this? Why didn't you tell me you'd captured a prisoner?"

"I wanted it to be a surprise." Zamora looked at Juliana. "You are surprised, aren't you, Señorita Julie? Perhaps you can tell us who our prisoner is."

"You know damn well who he is," Juliana said. She looked up at Brian. "Hello, Mr. McNeely. Welcome to the revolution."

"You bitch." The words were low. The lips were drawn back from his strong white teeth, threatening, wolflike.

"Alejandro," Zamora's voice was gentle. "Teach our guest some manners."

"Of course, *mi jefe*." The blow to Brian's stomach came fast and hard. He doubled over, then stood erect. Sweat beaded his forehead and he didn't speak until Rafael began to cry. Then he said, "Who're you trying to impress, Zamora? A five-year-old kid? Get him out of here."

"Yes, please," Maria said in a frightened voice. "Let me take Rafael to his room."

Zamora jerked his head in the direction of the door. "Very well, take Rafael and leave." He looked at Juliana. "You don't mind staying, do you, my dear? Or will it bother you to witness my attempts to question Mr. McNeely, since he's an old friend of yours?"

Juliana looked at Brian. His face was raw with pain; his eyes were on fire with hate. She dug her nails into her palms. She made herself turn away from Brian and look at Zamora. "To question or to brutalize?" she asked coldly. "You've been planning this all through dinner, haven't you, Zamora? What did you expect me to do, rush to his side and throw my arms around him?" She picked up her glass of wine and took a sip. "I made a decision today." She looked at Emilio and forced a smile to her lips before she took another sip of wine. "I'm sorry to disappoint you, Señor Zamora, but what happens to Mr. McNeely doesn't really concern me anymore. Brutality, however, does.

It sickens me, as it sickens anyone with a streak of decency in them."

Juliana stood up and pushed her chair back. "I find this whole thing gross, boring and juvenile. So if you'll excuse me I'm going to go find Rafael and Maria. We all need a breath of fresh air." She didn't look at Brian. She leaned down and kissed Emilio's cheek. "I'll see you later," she said.

The hardest thing Juliana ever did in her life was to walk out of that room. Her back was straight, her chin was up. She walked blindly, one foot in front of the other, a terrible set expression on her face, all the way to her room. Once inside she closed the door and leaned against it. Her eyes were closed, her body wet with perspiration. Then she staggered to the bathroom and was painfully, retchingly sick.

Juliana lay on the floor, her face against the tiles, and wept weak, silent tears that came from the very depths of her soul. Never, for as long as she lived, would she forget the expression on Brian's face when he had looked at her tonight. Oh God, how she'd wanted to rush into his arms, to stand beside him, fight beside him. For a moment she almost had, then from somewhere inside her a cold, calm voice warned her. She knew she could never help him if she did that. She could only help him if she pretended not to care—pretended to be one of them. But oh, what the pretending had cost.

At last Juliana got up. After removing her clothes, she got into the shower and stood under the cool wa-

ter until the sickness passed. Then, her mind clear, she
began to plan how she would help Brian escape.

The shed Brian was locked in was dark except for
the light of a half moon that came in through the slats
of the windows, making a shimmering path of light
across the dirt floor. Not unlike the path of gold on the
water the night he and Julie had gone swimming. He
remembered the way she had looked and for a moment he'd felt as though a giant fist had gripped his
heart and squeezed it. He'd been so filled with love
that night, a love that went beyond the physical, a love
that went soul deep, a love—God help him—that he'd
thought would last forever.

Groaning aloud, Brian ground his fist into the dirt
floor. Nothing had ever hurt him as badly as he'd been
hurt tonight. The blows he'd suffered had no impact
compared to what he felt when Julie had looked at him
with cool, expressionless eyes. Then she'd kissed Emilio Martinez and he'd suffered the pain of knowing
that nothing that had passed between himself and Julie had been real.

Brian's hands were tied behind his back. He struggled to a sitting position and tried not to think about
Julie. He had to figure a way out of here. He wasn't
sure what they planned to do with him, but he didn't
think Ricardo Zamora would let him leave alive.

But he would leave, Brian vowed, and when he did
he'd take Julie with him. He didn't give a damn about
the rebels or the revolution. He didn't even give a
damn about her now. But he would, by God, get her

out of here and back to the safety of her own country. Then he'd be finished with her forever.

It was a long time that night before Brian was able to sleep. When he did he dreamed of Julie, of that night on the beach when he'd carried her into their hut and laid her down on the straw mats. He dreamed of her body under his, of her softness closing around him. He moaned aloud in his sleep and awoke shaking and covered with sweat. Then, through the pain of his desire, he felt the ground move as it had moved one day on the beach. He heard a rumble, deep within the earth, then a roar. He looked up through the narrow slats of the window and saw a bright orange flame shoot high into the sky.

My God, Brian thought, it's the volcano. The damned volcano's erupting!

He lay watching the flames, listening to the rumble slowly subside. It wasn't going to blow tonight, he told himself. But it was going to blow, and when it did it would take everything on this side of the island with it.

Brian chuckled, a low, unpleasant sound in the small enclosed space. "Damn," he muttered, "if Zamora and his bunch don't kill me, the volcano probably will."

The volcano awakened Juliana too. She sat up in bed, then ran to the window. She looked out and saw the moon, and gasped when she saw the flames leap up that seemed almost to consume it. The ground moved beneath her feet again, while the bright orange flames grew higher and higher. She heard people shout. Footsteps pounded on the porch. Startled voices cried out. She clung to the side of the window, undecided whether to run or to stay where she was.

The flames receded; the earth steadied. Still Juliana stood, looking fearfully out into the night. When she heard Maria's voice crying, "Julie, Julie, are you all right?" she ran to the door to let Maria and Rafael in.

"Thank God, you're here," Julie said. "I was so frightened. Shouldn't we get out of here?"

"I don't think so." Maria hugged Rafael close. He whimpered in his sleep and she said, "It's all right. Go to sleep, Rafa. Go to sleep, darling." She laid him down on Juliana's bed. "It's only Manitura," she told Juliana. "He'll simmer down in a little while."

"Only Manitura! The volcano's going to erupt! We're almost directly below it. We've got to get out of here." A chill ran down her back. Brian! Dear God, Brian was locked up somewhere here in the camp. If anything happened he'd be trapped, unable to run.

"We'll have to leave if it erupts again," Juliana said, fighting to speak calmly. "Everybody will have to get out of the range of the volcano. That means Brian McNeely too, Maria. We've got to get him out of here before the volcano erupts. He's locked up... helpless. If anything happens we've got to help him."

"Nothing's going to happen." Maria avoided looking at Juliana. "The volcano isn't as dangerous as it seems. It kicks up every once in a while, then it goes back to sleep for another ten or twenty years."

Maria gestured to the window. "You see, already Manitura has calmed down. He may rumble a bit for a week or two, but believe me, there isn't going to be any big eruption." She glanced at Juliana, then away. "We can't help Mr. McNeely, Julie. His fate will be decided by Emilio and Zamora."

"Even if Zamora decides to kill him?" Juliana bit her lip in frustration. She knew that she had to go slowly, to try to find the words to make Maria help her. She took Maria's hand. "You don't *know* that the volcano isn't going to erupt. What if it does? How can you expose Rafael to that kind of danger?" She sat next to Maria and looking at Rafael sleeping so peacefully said, "If we free Brian he'll get us out of here." Juliana touched Maria's hand. "Please," she said. "Please help me free him."

"I can't." Maria pulled her hand away and stood up. "Zamora's a dangerous man, Julie. He won't let anything or anyone stand in the way of the revolution. What he did tonight—bringing Mr. McNeely into the dining room that way—was barbaric. He wanted to see you squirm, Julie. He wanted to see if you would run to that poor man." Her voice lowered. "I'm surprised you didn't. I thought you were in love with him."

"I thought so too," Juliana made herself say. "But whether or not I love him has nothing to do with wanting to help him."

Maria picked Rafael up. "I'm sorry," she said. "I'd help you if I could. But I can't." She didn't look at Juliana. "Perhaps after all Mr. McNeely will convince Zamora that he doesn't know anything. Perhaps he'll be set free.''

"Yes, perhaps.'' Juliana's voice was cold. She kissed Rafael's brow, then closed the door and leaned her back against it. All of her thoughts were on Brian.

She fought the tears that threatened to fall. Tears wouldn't help, she had to plan. She had to find a way to help him.

Juliana was still standing with her back against the door when someone knocked. It's Maria, she thought. She's changed her mind, she's going to help me. But when she threw the door open she saw that it was Emilio.

"Are you all right?'' he asked. "I tried to get here sooner but I was held up by Zamora. Old Manitura hasn't been that ferocious in years.'' He put his arms around her. "You must have been frightened, Julie.''

"Yes, I was.'' She stepped out of his arms. "Emilio, I have to ask...did you know that Brian McNeely had been captured?''

Emilio shook his head. "If I'd known I would have told you, Julie.''

"What's going to happen to him?''

"Zamora will try to get information from him, who he is, why he came to San Benito.'' He put his hands on Juliana's arms and turned her so that she faced him. "You still care about McNeely, don't you?''

"No,'' she said, a shade too quickly. "But he...he was Tim's friend, Emilio. I'd hate to see anything happen to him because of that. The idea of turning him over to Zamora and Miguel Otero sickens me.

They'll try to beat information out of him. They'll do whatever they have to do and then they'll kill him."

"I'll stop them if I can, Julie, and I'll talk to McNeely. I'll try to get him to tell me what he knows." Emilio's face was troubled. "But so much is at stake. We can't let one man stand in the way of what we hope to accomplish. McNeely knows where we are. He probably knows how many of us are here, what arms we have. If he gets away, if he goes back to the States, or to Sanchez-Fuentes with the information..." Emilio shook his head. "We can't let that happen, Julie. We can't take that chance."

Juliana knew that what he said was true. He didn't like it, but he'd do what had to be done for the sake of his country. As much as he might hate it, if he thought Brian endangered the revolution, he would stand aside and let them kill him.

But she wouldn't let them. Tomorrow she'd find out where Brian was being held. Tomorrow night she'd help him escape. Nothing, no one, would stop her.

Again in the night she heard the rumble of Manitura. Again she thought of the man fate had torn from her and lay awake until the morning sun streaked the sky.

Chapter 12

It was Juan Garcia who unwittingly led Juliana to the place where Brian had been incarcerated. She hadn't had the opportunity to speak to Garcia since the night he had rescued her from Miguel Otero. Once the big, bearded man had saluted her and said, *"Hola, muchacha,"* before he turned back to the men he was training. Last night when he'd come into the dining room with Brian he'd glanced at her, then away, and she'd had the feeling that he didn't like what he was doing.

The air was hot and muggy this morning. There seemed to be a stillness in the surrounding jungle. Even the birds and the usual querulous monkeys were silent. Khaki shirts clung to the backs of guerrillas. Men swore at each other. From time to time they glanced up at the volcano, frowning, worried.

When Juliana stepped out onto the porch, dressed in a pair of Maria's shorts and a T-shirt, she saw Juan speaking to several other men. When the men walked away he came over to Juliana and with a shy grin said, "*Buenos días*, Señorita Julie. You look tired this morning. Did Old Manitura keep you awake?"

"He scared the life out of me. Does he rumble like that very often?"

"He hasn't even breathed for the last twenty years or so, but the last few days he seems to be flexing his muscles." Juan shook his head. "I can't say that I like it, being this close to him, I mean. If he decides to let go we're in a dangerous position."

"That's what I thought last night." Juliana glanced up at the now quiet volcano. "Couldn't we move to another camp until the volcano quiets down?"

Juan shook his head. "Zamora wouldn't move unless he thought the danger was imminent. We have a lot of men, guns, equipment, it would be a tough job to move everybody and everything."

"But if lives are in danger..." Juliana let the words hang in the air.

Juan frowned. "I know." He looked up at the volcano again. "If it decides to blow we won't stand much of a chance of getting away." He looked at Juliana and his rough face softened. "But you should get away, Señorita Julie. You don't belong here; you've nothing to do with our revolution. This war we fight against our government isn't a pleasant war. We must do things we don't always like." Juan shook his head. "I'm sorry about what happened last night. There wasn't any call to bring the prisoner into the dining room. If they have to question him they can do it over there.'' He gestured toward a small shed just at the edge of the trees.

Juliana's breath caught. She wanted to rush to the shed, but with an effort to keep her voice steady she asked, "Have they... has anyone questioned him today?"

Juan nodded. "Otero and another man went to the shed early this morning. They came out thirty minutes later looking angry. So I guess the poor bastard didn't tell them anything."

Juan didn't see the paleness in Julie's face because he'd looked toward the shed. With a shake of his head, he said, "I don't like this sort of thing, taking prisoners, forcing them to talk. It isn't worthy of us." Then he sighed and said, "I must get back to work, Señorita Julie. It's been nice talking to you."

He saluted again but before he could turn away, Juliana said, "I haven't thanked you for rescuing me the other night, Juan. If it hadn't been for you I don't think I could have gotten away from Otero."

"He's a *cabrón*," Juan said vehemently. "I've warned him to stay away from you. If he even looks at you again, you tell me and I'll see that he never looks at another woman for the rest of his worthless life."

He left Juliana then, near the steps of the porch. She gazed out toward the edge of the jungle. The sun had shifted and was shining down on the shed where Brian was held prisoner. The heat must be intense; by noon it would be insufferable. A knot of pain gathered in Juliana's throat, and again she wanted to run to him. But she would have to wait until dark. Hold on, my darling, she thought. Hold on, Brian.

It had been bad this morning. The first time Otero hit him, Brian had lashed out with both feet, catching Otero in the stomach, knocking him to the ground. Hands tied behind his back, Brian had rolled, and when the other man grabbed him he'd lashed out again and kicked him in the hip. They'd both jumped him then. They'd held him down and pummeled him until he was only semiconscious.

"Enough," the other man finally said. "Zamora told us to question him, not kill him. Leave him be; we'll come back tonight."

"I'd like to finish him off right now." Otero spat. Then he drew back his foot and viciously kicked Brian. "That should hold you until tonight when we question you, *gringo*," he snarled. "Make no mistake, tonight you'll tell us everything we want to know."

They'd left Brian alone then, alone with his pain and his anger. He lay for a long time before he hunched himself up to a sitting position.

By midafternoon the heat in the shed was unbearable. Brian's throat was parched and dry. Just when he thought he could no longer bear his thirst, one of the men who had taken him into the dining room last night opened the door. It wasn't the man who had hit him, but the other one, the big one.

"*Dios*, but it's hot in here!" The man looked around the shed. "What are they trying to do? Let you die of the heat and of thirst?" He held a can of water to Brian's lips. "I'll leave the door open while I'm here so you can get more air," he said. "I'm going to untie your hands so you can eat, but don't try anything, eh? I'm just as strong as I look, and you don't look like you're in any shape to put up much of a fight."

Juan untied Brian's hands and handed him the plate of beans and a biscuit. He sat back on his haunches and looked at Brian. "They knocked the hell out of you this morning, didn't they? Do you think anything is broken?"

"If there isn't it won't be Otero's fault." Brian spooned some beans into his mouth as he watched Juan Garcia. He wondered if he could take him and decided he couldn't, not in the shape he was in. But he wanted to keep the big man here, as much for the air that came in through the open door as for whatever conversation or information he might get. "I heard the volcano last night," he said. "I thought it was going to blow."

"So did everybody else."

"I'm surprised you don't move out."

"Zamora won't move unless the whole mountain blows up." Juan scratched his beard. "We've got too many men, too much equipment. We..." He glared at Brian. "What in the hell am I telling you for? You're CIA."

"I'm not CIA," Brian said. "Damn it, I've tried to tell anybody who'll listen that I'm not. I came to San

Benito to question Emilio Martinez about the murder of Tim Thornton in Miami. I—''

"Thornton?" Garcia looked shocked. "Maria's husband?"

"That's right."

"I'll be damned!" His face puckered in a frown. "The Señorita Julie's name is Thornton. Maria's husband was her brother?"

Brian nodded. "She and Emilio knew each other in Miami. She's here now because of him."

"Yeah, I guess that's true all right. Zamora said they were engaged. That's why she's with us now, because of Emilio."

Brian gripped the tin spoon. He didn't look at Garcia because he was afraid that what he felt would show in his eyes.

"They kept her locked up the first night," Garcia said. "Then I guess she and Emilio got together and patched things up. She has the run of the camp now." Garcia stood up. "I'd better get back. You finished with the beans?"

"Yes, thanks."

"There's enough water to last you for the day. I'll be back in the morning." He stepped closer to Brian. "Hands behind your back," he said. "I've got to tie you up again."

"Couldn't you tie my hands in front of me? The water isn't going to do me much good if I can't reach it."

"No, I don't suppose it will." Juan grasped Brian's hands and tied them in front of him. He hesitated as he stood up, then said, "If you can convince them you're not CIA it might not go so hard on you. But on the other hand, everybody likes Emilio. They might not take too kindly to your wanting to arrest him for murder."

"I don't want to arrest him, I just want to question him."

"They might think it's the same thing, *gringo*. I sure as hell wouldn't want to be in your shoes." He went to the door, started out, then turning back said, "I'll come along tonight when Otero questions you. Maybe I can keep him from killing you."

Brian stared at the door after the big man closed it. "If I'm here tonight," he said under his breath.

Garcia had taken the plate away, but he hadn't seen the spoon that Brian had shoved behind him in the dirt. Brian took the spoon now. He searched the ground until he found a stone, then he went to work, scraping, sanding, rubbing, trying to sharpen it so that he would have some kind of a weapon for when they returned.

A little before lunchtime Juliana wandered into the kitchen. The cook, a dour-faced woman in her fifties, frowned at her but didn't refuse when Juliana asked for a cup of coffee. The woman poured the coffee, plunked the mug down on the table and stalked out, mumbling something about killing chickens for dinners.

Juliana waited. When she was sure the woman was gone she got up and began to look in the cupboards.

She found a plate of last night's biscuits and took three of them. She looked into an earthenware crock and discovered half a ham wrapped in cloth and a large round of cheese. Quickly, scarcely daring to breathe, she looked for a knife, cut some of the ham and the cheese and replaced what she hadn't taken in the crock. She hastily found a cloth napkin, wrapped the biscuits, the ham and the cheese together with the knife, and left the kitchen as fast as she could.

As Juliana passed from the kitchen into the corridor leading to the living room she paused to pick up several toy cars that Rafael had dropped. She put them on a chair next to a small knapsack that he had used to carry his lunch in when he was in play school. Glancing quickly around, she stuffed the things she'd stolen from the kitchen into the knapsack and closed it just as Alejandro Espinosa stepped into the hall.

"What are you doing?" he demanded.

"Picking up Rafael's toys." Juliana gathered up the toy cars and stuffed them into the sack. Forcing a smile to her lips she said, "Small boys aren't known for picking up after themselves, I'm afraid."

"I suppose not." Alejandro stared at her suspiciously.

"Well..." She tried to keep her voice steady, her hands from shaking. "If you'll excuse me I'll go find him." She turned and walked the other way, trying to be casual, trying to keep from breaking into a run. When the knapsack was safely hidden in her room she went looking for Rafael to suggest they go for a walk.

"I'll show you the barn," he said, and taking Juliana's hand led her out to the old red building at the edge of the jungle. "Here are my cows," he told her when they were inside. "Mama says they're mine, so I can have milk every day. This one's Mildred, the other one's Mabel."

"How do you do, Mildred and Mabel," Juliana said. Then while Rafael ran ahead to show her something else she looked around to see what she could find that might be of use. At a makeshift worktable she found a short crowbar. Quickly, keeping one eye on Rafael, she stuffed it inside her shorts against her hip and covered the slight bulge with her arm before she hurried to join Rafael.

Juliana saw the canteen when they were leaving the barn. She took it down and dusted it off, but knew she couldn't carry it out without somebody looking at her suspiciously. "Hey," she said to Rafael. "Wouldn't this be fun to take on a picnic?" She draped it over his shoulder. "You look like a real camper."

"Can we go on a picnic today?" he said.

"I don't see why not. We'll ask your mom to go too, okay? And we'll see if the cook will make us some sandwiches. Why don't you run ahead and tell your mom?"

Juliana watched him skip off, the canteen bouncing against his small body.

That afternoon the three of them followed a path through the jungle to a clearing. There, beside a small waterfall, they spread the blanket Maria had brought. For a little while Juliana almost forgot where she was or why she was here. In spite of the heat it was cool beside the small pond and the waterfall. She chatted with Maria, happy to be friends again. There was no rebel camp, no revolution. The air was warm with promise. Yellow butterflies darted among the flowers and birds sang in the trees above. They laughed as they watched Rafael try to catch a fish with a branch and a hairpin and ran to pull him out of the water when, frustrated over not catching a fish, he waded in to catch one with his hands.

After they'd eaten the sandwiches and drunk the lemonade they lay down on the blanket and looked up at the clouds above the trees, while Rafael fell asleep with his head on Juliana's shoulder. The two women talked of earlier days, and for a while at least, the harshness of reality was forgotten.

When they left the small clearing Juliana took the canteen and began to plan how and when she would help Brian to escape.

That night at dinner Juliana was quiet. Most of the conversation concerned Manitura and whether or not there would be other rumbles. Zamora insisted the volcano would soon quiet down. Alejandro, who Juliana realized was Zamora's right-hand man, agreed. So did Miguel Otero. Only Emilio expressed his concern.

"At least let's send Rafael and the women to safety," he urged.

"There's no danger," Otero scoffed as he poured himself another glass of wine. "I was born here at the foot of Manitura. Every once in a while the old man rumbles, but it means nothing." He downed the glass of wine and poured himself another before he looked over the rim of his glass at Juliana. "Soon I'll visit the *gringo*," he said with a sly grin. "Tonight he'll tell me everything I want to know. If he doesn't I'll—"

"You'll what?" Zamora's voice was angry. "Kill him? You do, Miguel, and I'll have your hide. The *gringo* won't be able to tell us anything if he's dead, so try to control yourself. If you can't, I'll send someone to question him who will."

"I'll control myself, *jefe*, but it won't be easy. I have no fondness for *gringos*." He reached out and grabbed Juliana's hand, and winking at her said, "Present company excluded, of course."

Emilio rested his fork against his plate. "Be very careful, Miguel," he said quietly. "The only reason you're alive tonight is because of Zamora. But even Zamora won't save you if you ever touch Juliana again."

Otero shrugged. "I have no more interest in *la señorita gringa*," he said. "She's all yours, and God help you, *compadre*, because I don't think she'll give you an easy time of it."

Juliana ignored him. When the conversation resumed she let it flow around her, anxious for the meal to be over, for darkness to come. In her mind she planned over and over again how she would free Brian, the way she'd put the crowbar between the hasp and the padlock. There wouldn't be time to say more than a few words. She'd give Brian the knapsack and the canteen. She'd say, *I love you, Brian, but I can't*

go with you. I can't leave Maria and Rafael. Later,
when this has ended, we'll be together.

She had to free him before Otero got to him again.

Dinner seemed interminable. Juliana barely nibbled at the food in front of her. She didn't touch the
wine. When Emilio said, "What is it, Julie? Aren't
you feeling well?" she said, "I have a headache, Emilio. It's so warm tonight, there doesn't seem to be any
air at all."

"You aren't used to the jungle climate yet. Would
you like to go to your room?"

"Yes, if you don't mind." She stood up, excused
herself and left the room.

When it was dark Juliana stood by the window. The
knapsack was packed, the canteen filled. She changed
from the dress she'd worn at dinner to a pair of dark-
blue shorts and a T-shirt.

Several men stood in the yard in front of the cabin.
Other men were gathered at the edge of a jungle. Juliana saw the flare of cigarettes, heard the buzz of talk.
She turned away from the window and began to pace
her room. She sat on her bed. She got up and checked
the knapsack again, then went to stand by the window. Unable to see the shed from where she was, she
prayed that Miguel Otero wasn't already there. Her
stomach tightened into knots at the thought of what
he might be doing to Brian.

By eleven o'clock the yard in front of the cabin was
empty. There was no sign of glowing cigarettes near
the jungle. Juliana slung the canteen and the knapsack over her shoulder. She felt the crowbar against

her hip. She slid one leg over the window sill, heard something and froze, not even daring to move.

Miguel Otero came out on the porch. He swayed and grabbed one of the wooden pillars for support, then straightened and with a chuckle slapped a leather strap against the side of his leg and headed toward the shed where Brian was held.

Juliana sucked her breath in. Once again she fingered the crowbar at her side, but before she could move the floor began to tremble beneath her feet and a roar that grew in intensity ripped through the quiet of the night. Suddenly the sky was lit by a bright orange flame that obliterated the moon and reached for the stars. Otero yelled and ran back into the cabin. Other men ran into the yard, frantic, bewildered, not sure whether to run or stay.

Quickly throwing a sweater around her to hide the knapsack and canteen, Juliana stepped through the window onto the porch. The yard was filled with terrified guerrillas pointing up to the orange flame. She commented as they commented, and when they turned to speak to someone else she slipped away from them and ran toward the shed. When she reached it she put her ear to the door, heard no sound, then softly called, "Brian? Brian, are you there?"

For a moment there was no sound. Then she heard, "Julie, is that you?"

"Yes, yes, Brian, it's me."

She took the crowbar out of her shorts and fumbled for the lock. When she found it she inserted the crowbar and jerked upward. Nothing happened. She tried again and skinned a knuckle. Almost weeping in frustration she tried again with all her strength, and suddenly with a snap the lock gave. She opened the door and stepped inside.

Brian loomed in front of her. By the fire of the volcano she could see his face, hard, tense, angry.

"Are you all right?" Juliana tried to put her arms around him but he stepped away from her. She saw the bruises, the cut over his face. "Oh God," she whispered. "What have they done to you?"

"Save the histrionics. Let's get out of here."

"No, I can't go." Juliana thrust the knapsack and the canteen toward him, then realizing his hands were tied, she reached in the knapsack and took out the knife. He held his hands out. She sawed through the ropes and when Brian was free he rubbed his wrists, trying to get the circulation back.

"Here." She handed him the knapsack and the canteen. "Everybody's distracted by the volcano. They won't see you if you hurry."

"You're coming with me," Brian snapped.

"No! No, I can't. I can't leave Maria and Rafael."

"And Emilio? You can't leave your fiancé?" Before Juliana could speak Brian grabbed her arm. "Come on!" he ordered. "We're getting out of here!"

"No, I..." She tried to hold back but he tightened his grip on her arm as he pulled her out of the shed. For a moment he looked around, then pulling her with him, broke into a run and headed for the jungle.

Chapter 13

Juliana had no choice but to follow Brian into the jungle. Behind them she heard the excited voices from the camp compound, in the trees above the frightened chatter of monkeys. She could see the flames from Manitura; the earth trembled beneath her feet.

Brian didn't speak as he dragged her along behind him, away from the camp in the direction of the volcano.

"Wait!" Juliana protested. "We can't go this way. We can't—"

"Shut up and run." His voice was harsh and he held her wrist tightly.

The air was filled with the acrid smell of sulfur. Bits of burning brush rained down on them stinging Juliana's arms and legs, singeing her hair. She was afraid, but there was no time for fear as Brian urged her on. Once she fell. Brian bent over her. His face, lit by the terrible orange glow shooting from the volcano, was hard with anger. "Get up!" he shouted. "Damn it, get up!"

Juliana stared at him, too shocked and frightened to protest when he jerked her to her feet. Her throat was dry with fear, of Manitura and of him. Her side hurt from running, her legs trembled with exhaustion. She wanted to scream to him to stop, to let her rest. She wanted to beg him not to look at her with such contempt. But there was no time, he wouldn't allow her the time.

They plunged on, climbing over rugged terrain. Brian jumped up on a rock and hauled Juliana after him. She felt the sharp pain of a skinned knee, but bit down hard on her lip and didn't cry out. He looked around, trying to get his bearings. Then he pointed upward and said, "That way."

"But the volcano..." Juliana looked up. "We can't," she protested. "We should head for the beach."

"That's the first place your boyfriend and his band of cutthroats will look for us. We go up and then we go back down to the jungle. *Then* we head for the beach. Meantime we say a prayer to whatever gods might be listening that Manitura doesn't erupt tonight. If it does this whole mountain's going to blow."

The earth shook beneath their feet. Juliana clutched Brian's arm to keep from falling. He steadied her, looked down into her face and for a moment his expression softened. Then he let her go and turned away.

Juliana followed him, up and up through the terrible night. Her face, her arms and legs were scratched by brambles. Her throat was choked by the acrid smell of sulfur. When she couldn't make it, Brian reached down and pulled her up to the next rock, and the next. Her chest was heaving with strain when he finally said, "We'll start down now."

If anything, going down was even harder than going up. The flames shooting up from the volcano weren't as bright now and there was only a half moon to guide their descent. Brian was below Juliana, guiding her to a foothold. But he didn't lessen his pace, even when, arms and legs trembling, she clung to the side of a giant rock and begged, "Please, Brian, let me rest. I can't make it. I can't..." Her voice trailed off into a sob.

Brian looked up at her. Her face was pressed tight against the mountain of rock, her fingers seemed embedded in the surface. He put a hand on her calf and felt her trembling with fatigue. He almost told her then how brave he thought she was, and that they had to keep going because by now the camp would know, Emilio would know that he'd escaped and that Julie was with him.

But with the thought of Emilio, whatever feeling of tenderness Brian had for Julie faded. She had betrayed him. For as long as he lived he'd never forget the sight of her sitting next to Emilio at the dining room table, or the way she'd dispassionately looked up at Brian. She'd barely flinched when the man Alejandro had struck him. Then as if bored, she'd given a polite little speech and left the room. But first she had kissed Emilio Martinez.

That kiss had wounded Brian as nothing else ever had. He'd barely felt the blows that followed. He'd smiled at the men who struck him and kept the picture in his mind of Julie kissing Emilio. The picture had given him strength; it had kept his hate alive.

He didn't know why Julie had helped him escape tonight. Perhaps she felt sorry for him. Perhaps the memory of what they had shared troubled her. Or maybe she thought of how her brother had died and had helped him because of Tim. But she hadn't *wanted* to escape with him. She'd wanted to stay in the camp with Emilio, to even die with Emilio if Manitura blew, rather than go with him.

Brian's hand tightened on her leg. "Come on," he said roughly. "You can make it. Ease your foot down. That's right. Steady, not much farther. Okay, you're on a ledge. You can rest."

Slowly Juliana released her grip on the rock's surface. Sweat ran down her body, her legs trembled so that she could barely stand. She turned her head to see how much farther they had to go and felt her stomach drop to her toes. With a gasp of fear she looked at Brian.

He handed the canteen to her. "Drink some water," he said. "It'll help your throat."

Juliana took it and drank, then handed it to Brian.

"Another fifteen minutes should bring us down to the jungle floor," he said. "I don't think your boyfriend will look for us in this direction."

"Brian..." Juliana tried to find the words to break through the terrible coldness of his voice, the hardness of his face. "Brian, about Emilio. He's not... It isn't the way you think between us. He—"

"I don't want to talk about it now, not here with you clinging to the side of a mountain." He put the canteen over his shoulder. "It really doesn't matter a hell of a lot to me what he is to you. All I give a damn about now is getting out of here alive." He glared up at her. "Follow me down if you can, Julie, or stay up here and cling to the mountain all night if you want to. It doesn't make much difference to me what you do."

Brian turned away from her and started his descent. Juliana stared after him. Quick tears rushed to her eyes, but she forced them back and grimly inched her way down. And down and down. Once she slipped, but Brian was there, in spite of what he'd said, to steady her.

They were almost down when it happened. Juliana looked down and saw the jungle floor less than fifteen feet below. We're almost there, she told herself. We've made it. A few steps more...

Her eagerness made her careless. She felt for a ledge and didn't hear Brian say, "Careful, that's not..." Then the ledge gave way under her foot and she fell backward, clawing the air for a support that wasn't there. The sound of Brian's voice echoed in her ears. "Julie! Julie!"

She hit the ground and rolled into a black and silent place.

Brian froze, then with a cry he climbed down, jumping the last five feet to the jungle floor. Julie lay on her stomach, lifeless, silent. Fear, like a large black beast, clutched at his heart.

He knelt beside her. With trembling fingers he felt for the pulse in her throat and almost cried aloud with relief when he felt its steady beat. Gently he rolled her over. He felt her neck, her arms. He ran his hands down her body to her legs and thanked God that nothing was broken. He sat down and eased her up in his arms. "Julie," he said. "Julie!"

Her eyelids fluttered. "I fell." Her voice wobbled. "I guess...I guess that's one way to get down in a hurry."

Brian couldn't help it. He pulled Juliana into his arms. He held her against his chest, his face buried in her hair, as he repeated her name.

Juliana didn't speak. She wanted to weep with the sweet relief of being in Brian's arms again. She clung to him. She put her face against his throat and let the tears come. He rocked her in his arms and she whispered his name and knew that nothing else mattered in this moment.

When at last Brian let her go he held her away from him and said, "Are you all right? Does anything hurt?"

"Everything hurts." Juliana attempted a smile. "I'm bruised and battered and my knees are skinned. I'm never even going to ever look at a mountain again." She gazed up at the volcano where only a thin flame still glowed in the night sky. "Is it over? Has it stopped?"

"At least for tonight." Brian stood and helped Juliana to her feet. "We'd better get out of here," he said. Then looking down at her he hesitated. Even though she'd said she was all right, the fall had shaken her. There were patches of fatigue under her eyes and the hand he held when he helped her up trembled.

"We'll find a place to rest soon," he said. He let go her hand and turned away.

Juliana followed, head down, helpless tears stinging her eyes again because the moment of brief tenderness had been lost. It'll be all right, she tried to tell herself. I'll make him understand that I had to pretend to be one of them so that I could help him. I'll tell him about Maria and Rafael, about not wanting to leave them. I'll explain about Emilio. She looked at him swinging through the brush ahead of her. But would he understand?

Thirty minutes later they came to a small clearing. Brian stopped and looked around, then he pointed to a low cluster of trees. "Over there," he said.

Juliana followed him, so weary she wanted to drop. When he put the knapsack down she sank to her knees and leaned her back against a tree.

Brian stamped the ground. "I'll be right back," he said. Juliana nodded without speaking as she watched him disappear through the trees. A few minutes later he returned with an armful of fern and moss. He knelt beside her and spread the ground with what he'd brought. "This ought to do," he said as he sat down and reached for the knapsack. "Hungry?"

"Yes. There isn't much there. I was afraid the cook would notice if I took too much food."

Brian looked at her, his brows drawn together, questioning. If she didn't care about him, why had she helped him? And if she did care about him why hadn't she wanted to escape with him? He handed her a biscuit. "There's some ham and cheese. Did you bring a knife?"

"I used it to cut the rope on your wrists. I must have dropped it. I'm sorry."

"It's okay, we'll manage."

They ate without speaking, and when they were finished they lay down together—but apart—there under the jungle trees. A night bird called, another answered. Then there was silence. Only silence.

Juliana was achingly aware of Brian beside her, so near, so far. She wanted to reach out and touch him, to tell him how much she loved him. But her eyes were heavy with sleep. I'll tell him in the morning, she thought. Then sleep came and took her thoughts away.

The night air grew chill. Instinctively they moved closer. Juliana's body was tight against him, seeking his warmth. Brian's arm was around her.

He awoke first and lay for a moment, uncertain where he was. He opened his eyes and looked up at the cover of jungle trees, of frangipani with fragrant blossoms, acacias and leafy palms. Birds sang, a curious monkey looked down at him, then cautiously began to peel a banana. Brian grinned, then stretched,

and when he did, Juliana murmured complainingly
and snuggled closer. Brian drew his breath in. He
looked at her, felt her warmth and her softness and
knew that he had to touch her. It didn't matter that
Julie had destroyed his love. He had to feel her
warmth. He had to....

Brian rested his palm against Juliana's breast. She
stirred. He cupped the roundness and his body swelled
with need. She sighed, then with a catlike stretch
moved closer into his embrace. He kissed her and her
lips softened and parted. His mouth was hard against
hers, his arms tightened possessively around her.

"Brian..." Juliana pulled back, wide-awake now,
her cinnamon eyes questioning. "Brian, wait. I have
to tell you, I have to explain—"

"No! No words, Julie, only this." He tightened his
hand on her breast. "And this." His mouth de-
scended on hers, covering her protests before she could
speak them. In this moment she belonged to him.
Later when she left him...

With a groan Brian rolled her under him. He covered her body with his and kissed her, deeply, pene-
tratingly, thrusting his tongue into her mouth, a
warning of what was to come. He heard her gasp of
protest, then she wrapped her arms around his neck.

But that wasn't what Brian wanted. This isn't love,
he told himself, this is only desire—raw, primitive desire. I want her now but when this is over... oh God,
when this is over... He raised himself and looked
down at Juliana. Her eyes were smoky dark, her lips
were swollen from the fierceness of his kisses. He

kissed her again and when she whimpered he took her
bottom lip into his mouth to suckle and sooth. He
kissed her until he became lost in the sweetness of her
mouth, her taste and her warmth. He felt her arms
around his neck, the yielding heat of her body and his
own body shook with need.

Brian let her go, pulled her to a sitting position, and
yanked the T-shirt over her head. She wasn't wearing
a bra and for a moment Brian felt a sob rise in his
throat because she was so damned beautiful. Her
breasts were small, but high and firm and perfectly
shaped. Her skin was soft, ivory tinged with pink gold,
and her nipples were the color of a ripe apricot—ripe
and waiting. He flicked his tongue against one, then
the other, and felt her quiver beneath him. He cupped
one breast and bent to suckle. The small tip was warm
and hard against his lips. He couldn't get enough, he
could never get enough.

He grasped Juliana's wrists in one hand and raised
them above her head so that her marvelous breasts
thrust upward toward his hungry mouth. He took one
raised peak into his mouth and reached for the other
and began to tug and roll the hard little nub between
his fingers.

"Brian," Juliana whispered. "Oh, Brian." Her
body arched to meet his lips as wave after wave of
pleasure swept over her. Half in fear, half in ecstasy
she offered her breasts to him, a feast for his pleasure. Small, wild sounds escaped from her lips, and
her body trembled and warmed with need.

"Please," she said. "Please, Brian, I can't stand any more." She tried to free the hands he held, to move away from the demands of his hungry mouth.

But he held her with his body while he gripped her wrists with his hand. "No." His voice was hoarse against her skin. "No, I want you to wait."

His teeth closed tight on one nipple and as Juliana cried out he heated it with his tongue. Then he freed her hands and rolling onto his side, brought her into his arms. He kissed her mouth. He caressed her, his hands warm against her skin. He touched the breasts he had suckled, running his fingers over their perfect roundness. He ran his hands down the smoothness of her back, over the flaring curves of her hips and knew that he had to feel his naked body next to hers.

"Wait." Brian moved away from Juliana just long enough to pull his clothes off. Then he lay down and took her into his arms again.

She gasped when she felt his nakedness, but he took her mouth again. His tongue prodded past her lips to find her tongue. He began again to caress her. He pressed his hand against the small of her back to bring her closer, then moved over her hip, between her legs. He touched her there and she felt the rasp of his breath in her mouth.

Juliana was lost now, a creature outside of herself, murmuring small hot words of desire as she moved closer to Brian.

"Touch me," he said against her lips. "Touch me, Julie." And when she did, softly, caressingly tender, he gasped with pleasure.

Her body was on fire with need, and she knew from her touch how much Brian wanted her. "Now," she whispered against his mouth. "Please, now."

He tore his mouth away from hers. But instead of releasing her he trailed a hot line of fire down her face, to her throat, her ear. He thrust his tongue into the hollowed curved and when she shook with pleasure he moved down her throat to find her breasts.

"No more. Brian, no..." She felt his teeth, his lips against her breasts. "I can't...darling...it's too much. I can't stand..."

"Tell me you want me." He moved up and grasped her chin. He kissed her mouth, his lips hard and fierce against hers. "Tell me," he repeated.

Juliana's body was ready to explode. "I want you," she cried. "Please, Brian. Yes, yes, I want you."

With a hoarse cry, Brian rolled her beneath him and entered her. He felt the hot moistness of her closing around him and his body thundered with pleasure against hers. She was his Julie now, and he was hers as she whispered his name and lifted her body to him.

Juliana was both devoured and devouring. Taking, giving, demanding as he demanded. She ran her hands up and down his body. She pressed against the small of his back to urge him closer as she lifted her body to his. She kissed Brian's shoulder, tasting, biting, healing with her tongue, surging with pleasure when he moaned against her skin.

He thrust deeper into her, frantic in his need, then slowed, afraid of hurting her. But Juliana urged him on. She held him close, lifting her body to his again and again and it was too much. "Now," he said against her lips. "Now, Julie."

Her body exploded with a feeling that threatened to shatter her. Up and up she spiraled, sure that she would spin right off the world. She sobbed his name against his lips and he took her cry into his mouth as together they spun into sweet nothingness.

When they opened their eyes again the sun filtered down through the trees. The sound of the birds was muted, softened. Juliana lay with her head on Brian's shoulder; his hand rested on her hip. She reached for his hand, and bringing it to her lips she kissed it. Then she pulled away from him so that she could lean on her elbow and look down at him.

"I want to tell you what happened. I know you don't understand how it was," she said.

"No, I don't want—"

Juliana put a finger against his lips. "The day that you left to go down to the dock to find passage for me, Maria called. I told her to come up to the room but she wouldn't. She was frantic and she started to cry. I ran down to talk to her. I told her you'd be back soon, that you'd help her, that you'd get Rafael away from them."

"Them?"

"Zamora. His men." Juliana took a deep breath. "But Maria wouldn't wait. I got into the car with her because I still thought I could talk to her, but she started driving and I didn't know what to do." She hesitated, wanting him to understand how she felt about Maria and her nephew. "Rafael is Tim's son,

Brian, he's like my own child. The thought of him being up there in the mountains terrified me.'' She looked down at Brian. ''Maria's a revolutionary. She loved Tim and she's fond of me, but she loves her country too.''

''What's Emilio to her?''

''He's Maria's cousin.''

''What is he to you?''

''He's a man I used to go out with. I don't love him, I love you. But he's a decent man who's trying to free his country from an oppressive government. I honestly believe he wants to do it without bloodshed. But I don't think men like Zamora and Miguel Otero want the same things Emilio wants. They're dangerous men, vicious men.''

Brian's eyes never left Juliana's face. He wanted to believe her, but there were too many unanswered questions, too many things that didn't add up. He shifted away from her. ''We can talk about this later,'' he said.

Juliana poked a finger at his chest. ''We're going to talk about it now, so shut up and listen.''

''Wait just a damn minute—''

''No, *you* wait just a damn minute!'' She glared at him. ''I went to the camp because of Rafael, *only* because of Rafael. Emilio's a nice guy, but he's not my guy. You are. And Zamora knew it, that's why he sent Maria to get me. He thought you'd come after me.''

Brian's eyes widened. ''But I thought—''

''No, you didn't think.'' Suddenly Juliana was just as mad as Brian had been last night. ''You just assumed that I'd walked out on you, that I'd gone to Emilio.'' She poked her finger at his chest again, harder this time. ''How could you possibly think I'd go from you...from your arms into his! What kind of a person do you think I am, you...you bum!''

Suddenly Brian wanted to laugh with relief because Julie looked so fierce, so ready to do battle. And because he loved her. But he didn't laugh because he knew if he did she'd sock him. So he lay back and put his hands behind his head, waiting.

''The first night I was there I tried to run away,'' Juliana said. ''Miguel Otero must have seen me slip away from my room because he came after me. He caught me in the jungle and he...'' She swallowed. ''He attacked me and he would have raped me if it hadn't been for Juan Garcia.''

''That son of a...'' Brian grasped one of her hands. ''If he hurt you, Julie, I'll kill him. I swear I'll kill him.''

''Juan arrived in time,'' she said. ''The next day, I decided to pretend that I believed in their cause. Emilio and Maria know I've always been a rebel, so I was able to convince them.'' Juliana looked down at Brian. She touched the side of his face and said, ''When Zamora had you brought into the dining room I wanted to run to you, Brian. I wanted to throw my arms around you and protect you from them. But I couldn't. So I pretended I didn't care, not even when Alejandro hit you.'' She lowered her head, reliving again that awful moment, and the way Brian had looked at her. ''The next day I found out where they had you and I began to plan how I could help you escape."

Brian took her hand. "Why didn't you want to come with me, Julie?"

"Because of Maria and Rafael. I didn't want to leave them behind."

"I see." Later, when he had time, he would call himself all kinds of a fool for the way he'd treated her last night. Now he wanted to hear the rest of it. "You said Maria was one of them, that she believed in the revolution."

Juliana nodded. "But maybe she'd leave if we could get her out of there, Brian. She knows how unhappy Rafael is. He's only a little boy, he shouldn't be in that kind of environment."

"But Maria's his mother, Julie. If she wants to stay there, if she wants to keep him there, there isn't much you can do."

"I know, that's why I decided to stay behind. That's why I didn't want to leave with you last night, Brian. It wasn't because I don't love you. I do, I—"

"I know, Julie." Brian pulled her down beside him and gathered her in his arms. He kissed the side of her face and said, "Julie I'm so sorry for the way I acted last night. I went crazy when I saw you at the cabin, when you kissed Emilio. When you wouldn't leave with me I thought it was because you wanted to stay with him." He kissed her again. "I'm sorry, Julie." He closed his eyes. "When you fell..." He shuddered and his arms tightened around her. "You were so tired. I should have let you rest, I should have helped you. Oh God, Julie, can you ever forgive me?''

"I love you," she said. "You didn't understand, you didn't know. There's nothing to forgive, Brian."

They held each other then and the wounds of the night were forgotten. Finally, because they were hungry, they sat up, and still naked, with only the birds and one curious monkey as an audience, they ate the biscuits and cheese and drank some of the water.

Chapter 14

Brian knew they should leave, that they needed every minute of the head start they had because of the near eruption last night. They'd head for the beach instead of the city, he decided, because by now word would have been sent to be on the lookout for both of them. He couldn't go to the police because it was very likely some of them were also involved in the revolutionary movement. He and Julie were on their own; his one concern was to get her to safety.

That might be a bigger job than he'd bargained for. He knew Juliana was determined not to leave the island without Maria and the boy. He'd have to convince her that Maria had every right to stay here if she wanted to, that Rafael was *her* son, not Julie's. If Maria wanted the boy to stay in San Benito, there was nothing Julie could do about it.

As for Brian, he had what he'd come to San Benito to get, he had Julie. If he'd moved fast enough Jack Kelly had the code book of the revolutionary movement. If it was in government hands then Brian had accomplished his mission. He had no idea what side the United States would take in San Benito's struggle, that wasn't up to him. Nor was he concerned any longer with Emilio Martinez. When he and Julie returned to Miami she'd go to see Jack and make an official statement clearing Martinez of any complicity in her brother's death. Then they could get on with their lives.

Their lives together.

He looked at Julie, who'd gone back to sleep after their meager breakfast. She was curled up under the tree, one hand under her chin, sleeping like a child. I love her, Brian thought as he looked at her. I love her softness, her passion, her sweet urgencies. I love her spirit.

She hadn't complained last night when he'd forced her to come with him, except for those first minutes when she'd tried to explain why she wanted to stay behind. But he hadn't listened. He'd thought Julie had betrayed him and he'd treated her like a criminal, a prisoner. Brian's face twisted in pain, remembering how he'd pulled her along after him, how he'd yanked her up on the rocks, then forced her to climb down. Once, when he'd ordered her to follow him down a particularly dangerous area, he'd put his hand on her calf to guide her and felt the trembling of her muscles. He knew that he'd pushed her beyond endurance, but he'd pressed her, made her move. And she'd fallen. Brian's eyes closed. He saw again that terrible moment when the rock crumbled under Julie's foot and she'd plunged to the jungle floor. His heart had stopped, and somehow he'd known in that moment that if she died his life would be over.

Julie. God, how he loved her.

She awakened a few minutes later to find that Brian wasn't beside her. She sat up and stretched, then moaned because every inch of her body ached. Her knees were skinned. One arm was badly bruised, her hips was sore. And she was hungry again. She opened the knapsack. There was a piece of ham and one biscuit left. She closed the knapsack and tried not to think about food.

Juliana was still trying to keep her thoughts from food when Brian came back. His arms were loaded with bananas.

"I found a dwarf banana tree," he said as he knelt beside her and handed her a banana.

Juliana took it eagerly. "How did you find it?"

"I saw our Peeping Tom monkey eating one, so I knew a tree must be around some place. I found something else, too. I'll show you as soon as you finish eating."

"That may be a while," Juliana said with a grin. "These are really great bananas."

Brian let her eat another one before he pulled her to her feet and said, "Come on, I want you to see what I've found." As he took her hand to help her up she smothered a groan. "Sore muscles?" he asked.

"Sore everything."

"I've got the remedy for that."

Juliana looked inquiringly at him, then let him lead her away from the clearing, deeper into the jungle. When Brian stopped she saw what looked like something out of a movie set somewhere in the Pacific. *Lush* was the only word she could think of to describe the scene. Green jungle trees, red and white hibiscus, magenta bougainvillea, orchids of every color, thick moss under her feet, a cascading waterfall and a spring pool with steam rising from the surface.

"It's a natural hot water spring," Brian said. "I thought you might like a bath."

"I'd love a bath." Juliana looked around her, and when she spoke her voice had fallen to a whisper. "It's so beautiful, Brian. It's like a miniature paradise."

"It is paradise," he said with a smile. "Right out of a forties movie. Any minute now Dorothy Lamour is going to come out from behind one of the trees dressed in a sarong."

"She'd better not." Juliana put her arms around his waist. "You're my guy and this is my fantasy." She removed her shirt and tossed it aside. "Let's go for a swim," she said.

Brian watched as she stepped out of her shorts and pulled the narrow band of satin panties down over her hips. He thought of the night on the beach when he'd wanted her to swim nude, of her hesitation and embarrassment. Now here she was, unashamed before him because she loved him. He cupped her face with his hands. "I love you," he said.

Juliana looked at him for a breathless moment. "Yes," she said, "I know." She stood on tiptoe and kissed his lips. "And I love you, Brian."

She waited while he stepped out of his clothes, then together they went down the mossy bank to water so deliciously warm she moaned with pleasure as it rose over her body. When they were waist deep they began to swim.

"This is wonderful," Juliana said as she looked around. "I could stay here forever."

Brian smiled at her pleasure, but he knew they couldn't stay much longer. Neither of them had mentioned the men from the camp who were searching for them this morning. They might have lost them by coming up over the mountain, but he couldn't be sure, he couldn't take that chance. As soon as they came out of the pool they'd gather up their things and go.

Juliana floated on her back. The sun filtered down through the trees, making drifting patterns of golden shade against her skin. Brian watched her for a moment, caught up in the wondrous perfection of her body, then he swam over to her. He ran his hands over her warm, wet breasts, then put his hands on her waist and helped her to stand. "You're beautiful," he said as he pushed her wet hair behind her ears and kissed her. "I wish we could stay here all day, but we've got to leave."

"I know." Juliana looked up at him. She put her hands on his shoulders, then ran them slowly down his back to his buttocks. "I love your buns," she said with a smile.

"My buns?"

She nodded. "Some women go for broad shoulders. I go for buns."

He directed a mock scowl at her. "If that's the case, when we're married I'm going to make you wear blinders when I take you out."

"When we're..." Juliana looked up at him. "Married?" she said.

"Damn right, lady. Do you think I've only been toying with your...?" Brian touched her breasts and grinned at her. "Your affections?" His face sobered. "I love you, Juliana. Will you marry me?"

"We're different," she hedged.

"As night and day."

"You believe in obeying the rules."

"True."

"I believe in breaking them if I think they're wrong."

"So I've heard."

"I won't change. I'll always stand up for whatever I believe in, even if it means spending a night in jail."

"I'll bail you out."

"I—"

Brian covered her mouth with his. Then, before Juliana could protest, he picked her up and carried her up to the mossy bank and laid her down. For a moment he didn't speak, he only looked at her, at the red hair turned to flame by the sun, the lovely fragile body, the perfect face, the eyes that grew smoky as he knelt beside her.

"I know we're different, Julie," he said. "I know there'll be times when we don't understand each other, when we're going to fight and argue. But we'll always make it up because we love each other." He kissed her. "The only thing I won't compromise about is marriage. We're getting married just as soon as we get back to Miami." He kissed her again. "Understood?"

Juliana took a deep breath. "Understood."

"I bought you a ring."

"What?" Her eyes were wide, startled. "When?"

"When we came back to the city from the beach at Tenango, the morning I went down to the dock to find passage for you to Belém."

Juliana stared at him. "The morning I went away with Maria," she said quietly, sitting up and leaning her face into his shoulder. "You bought me a ring and when you returned I was gone. Oh Brian, I'm sorry." Her voice was muffled.

He rested his hand in her hair, holding her, soothing her, and whatever doubt she may have had about marrying him fled. Whatever their differences, she and Brian belonged together. There would never be another man for her.

Lifting her face to look at him, she asked, "What kind of a ring?"

"A ruby. I saw it in a shop window. If you don't like it—"

"Of course I'll like it." She touched his face.

"Did you bring it with you?"

Brian shook his head. "No, I left it back in the room. I was so upset when I found you missing, so afraid that something had happened to you, that I just tossed it into a dresser drawer."

He still remembered how he'd felt when he'd walked into that empty hotel room and she wasn't there. He'd been terrified, then angry, then terrified again. And he'd picked up her white gown and held it against his face, breathing in the scent of her perfume, feeling hollow inside, lost without her. Now with a sigh he drew Julie into his arms. "I love you," he said. Then he kissed her gently, ashamed that he had taken her too fiercely last night. He wouldn't do that today. Today would be all for Julie.

She wrapped her arms around his neck when he rained soft kisses on her face and her ears. His tongue felt warm against her skin, and the hands that held her breasts to his lips were gently caressing. He lay down beside her, and Juliana sighed, savoring every touch, every flick of his tongue.

Like a blind man, Brian memorized the curves and lines of her body, savoring where her skin was the softest, the tenderest. Lovingly he traced his fingers over the indentation of her waist, the flare of her hips. His mouth followed the path of his hands down to her waist and across her belly, loving the scent of her, reveling in the texture of her skin.

Juliana quivered with excitement as her body warmed anew to his touch. She pressed her hands against the small of his back to draw him closer, but Brian held back. He wanted this time between them to last, for never again would they return to this perfect place. Their bed was soft green moss, their cover the blossoming trees and the sky. Julie was his—and he was hers.

He leaned back and looked at her. He ran his hands over her body again and when she asked him to make love with her he shook his head and said, "Not yet, love. But soon, very soon."

He kissed her again, then began to move slowly down her body. His tongue, like a fiery weapon, burned and teased until her bones were weak with longing and the pulse beat wildly in her throat.

Juliana touched him and he moaned aloud. But when she tried to merge her body with his, Brian said, "Not yet, sweetheart."

He parted her legs and nipped the tender skin of her inner thighs. When she held his wrists he begged her not to stop him. He had to touch her.

His touch turned the blood in her veins to liquid fire. Her body trembled as incoherent cries of pleasure tumbled from her lips. Brian reached for her breasts, taking the ready peaks in his fingers and all the while his sweetly relentless mouth drove Julie further and further toward that final breaking point.

"Brian..." Her voice was a low, keening protest as he pushed her beyond what she could bear. She clutched his shoulders, biting her fingernails into his skin. If he didn't stop he would drive her beyond the point of control. He would... Suddenly the world began to slide and spin. Sky merged with earth and with her as she spiraled faster and faster into unreality. She cried Brian's name. She clung to him and sobbed aloud when he lifted himself over her and joined his body to hers.

"Look at me, Julie," he said softly.

Brian's face was so full of love. She touched his cheek. "Darling," she whispered. "Oh, darling."

Still looking at her he began to move deeper into her body, and when he did that wonderful, frightening, out of control feeling began again. Juliana raised her body to his, offering herself, giving as well as taking, her heart so full, her body so alive that it was almost past bearing.

Together, wrapped in love, they climbed higher and higher until they reached that wonderful peak, reached that boundary that only lovers know and others seek but rarely find.

Juliana took his cry into her mouth and she tightened her arms around him, filled with the wonder of the moment and with a love that went beyond words.

They lay together when it was over, hearts and bodies close, there on that bed of moss in their brief Eden.

When finally their breathing slowed and steadied, Brian said, "We have to go soon."

"I know." Juliana looked up through the trees where the clouds, like puffs of cotton candy, drifted in the blue sky. She raised herself on one elbow and looked down at Brian. His face was relaxed. All of the tension and strain of the night before had disappeared. He still showed the marks of his imprisonment, but the bruises were fading, the cut on the side of his head was healing. She touched a bruise on his side, then leaned to kiss it and felt his skin quiver under her lips.

He helped her up and once more they went into the pool. When they came out they dried their bodies with his shirt, then dressed and filled the knapsack with bananas, and the canteen with water from the waterfall.

Hand in hand they left the clearing. Only once did Juliana look back. When tears came to her eyes, Brian put his arm around her, understanding her sense of a paradise lost. Then he took her hand and together they walked into the jungle.

At noon they rested. The air was hot and still. "Old Manitura has gone back to sleep," Juliana said. "Let's hope he sleeps for another hundred years."

Brian looked up at the volcano. "I have a feeling he's going to blow long before that." He got to his feet. "I'll feel a hell of a lot better once I get you off this island." He picked up the knapsack. "If we're going in the right direction we should reach the beach before nightfall. From there we'll..." He stopped, frowning as a sudden flight of birds flew from the trees above their heads.

"We'll what?" Juliana asked.

"Shh." Brian's hand tightened on hers. He pulled her back into the shadow of the trees.

Juliana's eyes widened with apprehension. She strained to listen. There was only silence. Then a shout. "Over here."

The breath caught in her throat. She looked at Brian, frozen and afraid.

"Come on," Brian whispered. He moved cautiously, quietly, urging her to keep low behind him. He silently called himself every kind of a fool for staying behind at the pool this morning.

Another voice called out. Brian pulled Juliana back farther into a shrub of trees.

"It's Miguel Otero," she whispered close to his ear. She felt paralyzed by fear, not for herself, but for Brian. She'd be relatively safe as long as Emilio was in charge. There'd be a scene, accusations, and they'd probably lock her up again. But none of them, except perhaps Otero if he had a chance, would harm her. But they would harm Brian. No one, not even Emilio, cared whether he lived or died. They mustn't get caught. Brian mustn't get caught.

Brian's face was tense as he looked cautiously around. The men were behind and to the right of them. Maybe they had a chance if they went forward. He got down on his hands and knees, and motioning Juliana down, pointed forward. She followed him, her heart racketing against her ribs.

The voices grew closer. Juliana wanted to get up and run, but made herself follow Brian. Once, when a man shouted close by, Brian put his hand in the middle of her back and shoved her flat to the ground. She lay there, her face pressed close to the earth, not daring to breathe or to move. She heard the thud of boots, the snap of underbrush close to where they lay. Finally the steps faded. Brian touched her arm and began to crawl forward.

Fifty feet. A hundred feet. Sweat trickled down Juliana's nose. Behind them voices called out. Brian stopped. She stopped. They waited. The voices drew closer. Brian got up and helped Juliana to her feet. "Run!" he whispered.

A shout went up. A shot rang out. She and Brian fought their way through the overhang of limbs and vines. A bullet whizzed over their heads. Brian pulled her to the ground, his arm protectively around her shoulders, trying to shield her. Before they could get up two men crashed through the trees.

Juliana looked up, past the rifle, into the narrowed, triumphant eyes of Miguel Otero.

The other men shouted, "We have them! Over here!"

Brian helped Julie to stand. Her face, in spite of the heat and exertion, was pale. He saw the rise and fall of her breasts and knew how frightened she was. He looked at Otero. Otero, too, was watching Julie, watching her the way a fat tomcat watches a mouse. Suddenly Brian found himself hoping, praying that Emilio Martinez was in the search party.

Six men ran toward them. Juan Garcia was in the ranks—so was Emilio.

"Julie!" Emilio ran to her. He put his hands on her arms. "Are you all right? My God, I went crazy with worry."

"I'm all right, Emilio."

"Thank God." He turned to Brian, his face twisted with anger. "How did you convince her to help you, McNeely?"

"She didn't help me." Brian took a step away from Juliana. "I caught her out in the yard when all hell broke loose because of the volcano. I forced her to come with me."

"He's lying," Otero said. "She helped him get away and she escaped with him."

"You're wrong, Otero. Julie didn't help me get away. You did."

"What in the hell are you talking about?" Otero raised his rifle.

"When you interrogated . . . is that the word for beating the hell out of me? When you interrogated me you dropped your knife. I managed to cut the ropes around my wrists and pry the hinges off the door. I slipped out into the yard while the rest of you were yelling about the volcano. I grabbed Julie. She fought like a wildcat, but I hit her and slung her over my shoulder. By the time she came to we were a couple of miles from the camp.''

Brian didn't look at Juliana. His voice was cool and impersonal. Almost imperceptibly he'd managed to move away from her.

"He's lying," Otero said.

"I don't think so." Emilio put an arm around Juliana. "It must have been terrible for you," he said. He looked at Brian. "I'd kill you right now, Mc-Neely, but there are a lot of questions we want answers to. But when we're finished with you..." Emilio let the words hang in the air. Then tightening his arm around Juliana he said, "Come on, darling, let's head back to camp."

"No!" Juliana pulled away from him.

"Julie!" Brian's voice was sharp, commanding.

"I'm sorry," she said to Emilio. "I—"

"Shut up!" Brian muttered.

Otero raised his rifle. "Keep your mouth shut, *gringo*," he said, and before anyone could stop him he hit Brian a terrible blow on the side of the head. Brian fell back and stumbled to the ground.

"Brian!" Juliana fell on her knees beside him. She cradled his head. She tried to wipe the blood from his face, then looked up at Miguel Otero and screamed, "If you touch him again I'll kill you!"

"What are you doing?" Brian whispered through the fog of pain that surrounded him. "You little fool. Without me you've got a chance."

"Not without you," Juliana said. "Never without you."

Emilio pulled her to her feet, his face set.

Juan helped Brian to stand. "Easy," he whispered, "or that *cabrón* Otero will kill you on the spot."

Brian nodded. He looked at Emilio. "All right," he said. "Julie helped me escape. But she didn't want to go with me, Martinez. She didn't want to leave Maria or the boy." He took a deep breath. "Or you. She said it was you she loved, not me. I forced her to come. I tried to force her to love me. I—"

Emilio raised his fist, but before he could strike Brian, Juliana said, "Emilio, don't." She put her hand on his arm. "I'm sorry. Brian's lying because he wants to protect me. I went with him willingly, Emilio, and I want to be with him now, no matter what happens."

No one spoke. Juan Garcia drew his thick brows together as he looked from Julie to Brian. Emilio's face was frozen and tense. Then he said, "Tie them," and turned away.

Chapter 15

Emilio led his men through the jungle. He moved fast; he spoke to no one. Their khaki shirts stuck to their backs and sweat rolled down their faces, but Emilio didn't slow his pace. Once Miguel Otero started to complain, but stopped when he saw the look on Emilio's face.

The last hour of the trek was torture for Juliana. The air was so hot and still she felt as though she couldn't breathe. It became an agony to put one foot ahead of the other. Her body ached. Her sweat-damp clothes stuck to her skin. She glanced at Brian once or twice and when she saw how concerned he looked, she tried to smile. Once she stumbled and fell, hard, because with her hands tied behind her back she couldn't break her fall. She lay face down on the jungle floor.

Leave me here, she wanted to say. I can't walk any more. I have to rest.

Brian ran to her side just as Juan pulled her to her feet. "It won't be much farther, *muchacha*," Juan whispered. "You've got to keep going."

"Untie her, Martinez," Brian said angrily. "She can barely stand, let alone try to get away. What kind of a man are you, doing this to someone you pretended to care about?"

"Pretended to care about?" Emilio swung around and faced Brian, his fists clenched, his nostrils white with anger. In a voice so low the others couldn't hear he said, "I loved her. I cared about her. In time, if it hadn't been for you, she might have loved me back."

"If you loved her why did you leave her?" Brian said.

"I had no choice. My country needed me." Emilio stepped back. "My country still needs me and I won't allow anything or anyone to stand in the way of what I must do."

"Not even Julie?"

It seemed for a moment that Emilio stopped breathing. "Not even Julie," he said at last.

When she stumbled again Juan took her arm. He held her up and helped her to walk until finally Emilio said, "All right, we'll camp here for the night." Then she sank down where she stood and rested her head on her knees.

"Julie?" Brian said. "Are you all right?"

She raised her head and looked at him. "Yes," she managed to say. "I just need to rest for a while. If I could have some water..."

"Here you are, Señorita Julie." Juan held a canteen to her lips, and when she finished drinking he held it to Brian's lips and whispered, "Your situation is serious, *señor*. You'll be lucky if you get out of this alive."

"I don't need you to tell me that." Brian looked down at Julie. Her eyes were closed, the damp hair clung to her forehead. "She's got nothing to do with this," Brian said. "She only came to San Benito because of Maria and the boy. Talk to Emilio, try to convince him to let her go."

"I don't think anyone can convince him of anything right now. Emilio's a good man, but his love for her has turned to hate because of you. Besides, *señor*, I've seen what is between you and the *señorita*. I doubt that she would leave you."

Brian swore under his breath because he knew what Juan said was true. Julie wouldn't willingly leave him. His only hope was to plead with Martinez to release her and force her to leave the country.

Brian watched Emilio and the other men. He had no quarrel with them or their revolution. If he had lived all his life under a dictatorship like Sanchez-Fuentes he'd have revolted a long time ago. And he, like these men, wouldn't have let anything or anyone interfere with the cause. Which didn't make him feel any better.

Brian eased his back against a tree. He knew his chances of getting out of San Benito alive weren't good, but he couldn't believe that Martinez meant to harm Julie. He looked down at her. Her face was flushed, her breathing shallow. She'd been through a lot these last few days, first with him, now with Emilio. It's strange and terrible, Brian thought, we both love her, yet we've both treated her badly.

But I never will again, Julie, Brian silently vowed. If we get out of this I swear I'll always show you the love you deserve. Then, because he had to hear her voice, he said, "Julie? Julie, are you all right?"

She thought she heard him speak, but it seemed to her that an answer would take more strength than she possessed. In this state between sleep and wakefulness she could almost forget the ache of the arms that were tied behind her, the burning pain where the rope cut into her wrists. She was half aware of the voices of the other men, of the smell of wood smoke, of bacon frying, but all she wanted to do was lie still with her eyes closed.

Juan squatted beside her. "I have your dinner," he said. "I'm going to untie you so you can eat."

She opened her eyes. Juan helped her sit up and freed her hands. "You'll feel better when you get some food into you." He rubbed her wrists. "Is that better?"

Juliana nodded, mumbling her thanks as she took the plate of beans and bacon from him. Through eyes glazed by fatigue she watched him release Brian.

"That's Alberto Moro who has his rifle trained on you," Juan warned Brian. "He's a good shot, so don't try to escape."

"We're not going anywhere." Brian took a bite of the bacon. "Is there any coffee?"

"Sure. I'll bring you a couple of cups."

"Gracias." Brian watched the big man amble over to the fire before he turned to Juliana and said, "You've got to eat, Julie."

"I know." She put a spoonful of beans in her mouth. "What do you think our chances are?" she asked.

"Not too good," Brian said truthfully. He looked at her. "That was a damn fool thing you did before. You wouldn't be in the situation you're in now if you'd shut up and let me handle it." He lowered his voice. "I love you for what you did, for being brave and wonderful, for loving me. But..." He shook his head. "But I won't let you do this, Julie. I want you to tell Emilio you're sorry. Beg, cry, do whatever you have to do to make him release you." Brian's voice held an edge of desperation. "Tell him if he lets you go back to Miami you'll wait for him there. Promise him anything you have to to get out of here. You have your whole life ahead of you. You—"

"I don't have any life without you, Brian. If we escape it will be together." She looked over to Emilio, standing near the fire, his back to his men. "I can't believe that Emilio will harm either one of us. He's not that kind of a man."

"He's a man who's in the middle of a revolution," Brian said. "His country's important to him; he's fighting for her survival. He has enemies in his own camp, men like Zamora and Otero. He's fighting for his life, Julie. He can't afford to let anything or anyone stand in his way." Brian put his plate down and reached for her hand. "Please, Julie, do what I ask. Save yourself."

Juliana moved closer and rested her head against his shoulder, not caring that the others in the camp saw them. "I can't," she said. "Not without you, Brian. Never without you."

Brian angrily started to speak, then stopped, so filled with love that for a moment no words would come. He put his arm around her. "All right, love," he said. "I won't ask again." But I'll speak to Emilio, he thought. He's got to let Julie go. He's got to.

They sat like that until Juan brought their coffee. Brian nodded his thanks, but remained silent, his mind a jumble of thoughts—thoughts of escape. He wouldn't give up, not as long as there was a chance. He and Julie were going to have a life together, and he'd do whatever was necessary to ensure it.

They reached the camp a little before noon the next day. As they neared the clearing Juliana heard Rafael call out to his mother, and knew that the little boy would see them as soon as they stepped out of the jungle. She stopped, then said to Emilio, "Can't you untie me now? Rafael is here. I don't want him to see me like this."

Emilio hesitated, then nodded to Garcia. "Untie her," he snapped.

Juliana rubbed her wrists together, then brushed her fingers through her hair, and forcing a smile stepped out into the clearing.

"*Tía* Julie." Rafael's voice was a squeal of delight as he ran toward her. When Juliana dropped to her knees to embrace him, he ran into her arms. "Where'd you go to?'' he asked. ''You didn't even say good-bye.''

''I hadn't planned on going, Rafa. That's why I didn't say goodbye.'' She looked past him to Maria, and getting to her feet said, ''Hello, Maria.''

''Julie?'' Maria looked at her disheveled sister-in-law, then at Brian. ''What happened?''

''She helped her *gringo* lover to escape and ran away with him,'' Miguel Otero said. ''Wait until I tell Zamora we've found them. He'll be overjoyed to see our *guests* have returned.''

But Zamora didn't have to be told. He'd stepped on the porch when he heard them, and now he quickly came forward. ''I see you found them,'' he said to Emilio. ''Good work. Throw them into the shed.''

Miguel grabbed Julie's arm, but before he could yank her away Rafael began screaming at him, ''Leave Julie alone. Leave her alone!'' He doubled his small fist and struck out at Otero.

''Darling, don't.'' Julie picked the boy up. ''It's okay, sweetie,'' she said. ''Emilio and Señor Zamora just want to ask me a couple of questions.''

''Who's he?'' Rafael pointed to Brian.

''His name is Brian McNeely and he's a very good friend of mine.''

''But why's he tied up? Was he bad?''

Brian grinned at the boy. ''No, Rafael, I wasn't bad. I just had a little disagreement with some of your friends.''

''That's enough.'' Emilio started to turn away. ''Get them out of here.''

"Hold on a minute," Brian said. "Lock me in the shed if you want to, but don't put Julie in there. The place is like an oven during the day, it'll kill her."

"She's not that fragile." Zamora laughed, then he snapped his fingers at Miguel and said, "Lock them up."

"No, please, Ricardo." Maria put her arm around Julie. "Let her come with me. I'll keep an eye on her, I promise."

"Take your son into the house," Emilio said harshly. Then he nodded to Miguel Otero. "Take them away. If the *gringo* gives you any trouble you have my permission to handle him as you like. As soon as you're finished come to the cabin."

"Emilio, please!" Maria begged as Rafael clung to Julie and started to cry.

Emilio glared at her. Then he picked the protesting Rafael up in his arms and strode toward the house.

Miguel gave Brian a shove. "Give me a reason to hit you, *gringo*," he taunted. "Just give me a reason."

"Take it easy, Otero," Juan cautioned. "Zamora and Emilio will want to question the prisoner. They can't do it if he's unconscious."

Otero glared up at the larger man, then backed off. "Your concern for the *gringos* is touching, Juan." Miguel pushed Brian ahead of him toward the shed.

Juliana's face was pale. She didn't expect mercy for herself; she knew there'd be none for Brian. Last night he had told her to ask Emilio for her freedom, to beg and to cry if she had to. She wouldn't do it for herself, but she would for Brian.

The door of the shed stood ajar, the doorjamb broken where Julie had pried it loose.

"Damn!" Otero exploded. "We can't put them in there."

"What about the room next to the stable?" Juan said. "The walls and the door are a foot thick. They'll never break out of there."

Otero hesitated, then with a shrug he said, "All right. We'll take them there." He didn't see the look of relief on Juan Garcia's face.

The room next to the stable wasn't the Waldorf, but it was better than the shed. There were straw mats on the floor, a bench, a table, three narrow windows high up on the walls. There was also a partition that hid a washstand and a toilet. Brian looked around and behind Otero's back, shot a grateful glance at Juan.

"It's too damned comfortable," Otero said.

"But the door's solid." Juan hit it with his fist. "It'll take more than a crowbar to get them out of here."

"Tie the woman's wrists," Miguel said.

"Why? She's not going anywhere. Neither is he." Before Otero could object, Juan untied Brian. "*Dios*, Miguel, how do you expect them to get a drink of water or go to the bathroom with their hands tied behind their backs?" He pushed Brian down on one of the mats, gave him a cautioning look, then said to Otero, "Come on, they're waiting for us at the cabin."

Otero muttered an obscenity as he followed Juan out the door. When it banged shut Brian said, "God bless Juan Garcia." He got up and looking at Julie, said, "Are you all right?"

"Better now that we're alone." Juliana put her arms around his waist. "This is my fault, Brian. If I hadn't left Miami...if you hadn't come to San Benito after me—"

"I'd have missed the best part of my life," Brian finished for her. He rested his chin on the top of her head. "I'd never have gotten to know who you really are," he said. "I'd never have fallen in love with you."

Juliana leaned back into his arms and with a weary smile said, "I loved you a long time before you loved me."

"Oh?" He lifted one eyebrow.

"In Miami. I knew the first time you kissed me that I loved you."

"But you wouldn't even give me the time of day. I called you dozens of times before you let me take you out to dinner. After that one time you wouldn't see me again."

Juliana nodded. "Because I didn't want to fall in love with you."

"That doesn't make any sense."

"I know." She reached for his hand. "What are we going to do, Brian?"

"We'll talk to Emilio."

"He won't listen. He hates us both. He—"

"Not you, Julie. In spite of what he says, Emilio's still in love with you. If I could talk to him, convince him that I didn't come to San Benito because of the revolution, I think we might stand a chance of getting out of here."

Juliana shook her head. "I don't think so, Brian. I think Maria's our best bet. If there's any way she can manage it, I'm pretty sure she'll try to help us." She rested her head on her knees. "Poor Rafael," she said. "This is terrible for him, he hates it here."

"Maybe we can convince Maria to come with us when we break out." Brian leaned back against the wall and drew Julie to him. *When* we break out, he thought, not if.

"Congratulations on finding them." Zamora sat behind the desk in the room that served as a study. He poured a splash of brandy for Emilio and one for himself. "I'm glad your eyes are finally open where the woman is concerned."

Emilio didn't answer. He took the brandy and drank it in one gulp, then closed his eyes and took a deep breath.

Zamora leaned across the desk. "She's trouble, Emilio. We have to get rid of her."

Emilio shook his head. "She has nothing to do with the revolution. She helped McNeely escape because she loves him. That doesn't make her an enemy."

"Doesn't it?" Zamora poured more brandy into their glasses. With a wave of his hand he said, "All right, we'll talk about her later. Now what about McNeely? He's CIA."

"Maybe. Maybe not."

"I'll question him." Zamora smiled. "I learned how to handle prisoners when I was with Sanchez-Fuentes. I'll make him talk."

"I'm not so sure. McNeely's tough."

"Which will make it all the more enjoyable." Zamora took a sip of his drink. "But it might take a little time." He drummed his long, thin fingers on the desk. "The way to do it would be through the woman. I don't think our Señor McNeely would stand by too long once she started screaming."

"No!" Emilio jumped to his feet and stared at Zamora. "You keep your hands off her."

"But why? I thought you no longer cared what happened to her." Zamora smiled up at Emilio. Then he shook his head and said, "You know what your trouble is, don't you, Emilio? You're too soft. You want the revolution, but you want it to succeed without bloodshed. I wasn't like you when I was your age, even then I knew that it's only the strong who survive in this world."

Zamora leaned back in his chair. "I don't think I ever told you that I went to the University of Havana when I was a young man. I didn't do too well the first year I was there. The studies were difficult, I made no friends, I was alone all the time. During the second year I joined a group of political activists and I took a course in political science. My professor was brilliant. He liked me, we became friends, and suddenly my life turned around because he opened up a whole new world of ideas to me. We talked about everything; my most pleasurable times were spent with him. We smoked Havana cigars and drank good Cuban rum and we talked. *Dios*, how we talked. He was more of a father to me than my own father had ever been.

"Then one night at one of my political meetings his name came up. 'He's our enemy,' the president of our club said. 'He must be gotten rid of.' I protested that the professor was a decent man, but the others said,

'His politics are not so decent, Ricardo. He must be dealt with.'

"It was decided that we would draw straws. The one who drew the short straw would kill my teacher."

Emilio stared at Zamora with growing horror. "You drew the short straw?"

"Yes." Zamora poured more brandy into his glass. "I arranged to meet him the next night near the embarcadero. There was a mist in the air and I saw him waiting for me under an overhang of roof." Zamora hesitated. "You must understand, Emilio, I didn't particularly like what I had to do, but I did it."

"You killed him."

Zamora nodded. "I walked up to him. He smiled. I said, 'Good evening, Professor,' and I shot him."

Zamora stood up and with his hands flat on the desk faced Emilio. "That's the kind of courage it takes for a revolution to succeed. When I'm president of San Benito I'll get rid of whomever I must. Anyone who disagrees with me will perish in the flames of revolution. When I am president..."

He went on, but Emilio didn't listen to the words, because words weren't important now. He knew what kind of a man Zamora was. "When I am president ..." Zamora said again.

It was at that moment that Emilio knew he must never allow that to happen. If he had been weak, now he would be strong. He'd do anything to prevent Ricardo Zamora, or anyone like him, from taking over his country.

His country, his San Benito.

Chapter 16

No one came near them that night. They bathed as well as they could, then lay down together on the straw mats. Juliana was tense, listening for a footfall that might mean someone was coming for Brian.

She reached out and took Brian's hand. More than anything else in the world, she wanted to keep Brian safe. He had become a part of her; she couldn't bear it if anything happened to him. She'd do anything she had to do to protect him.

She had to talk to Emilio. In spite of everything that had happened, Juliana believed he was a decent man. If she could convince him that Brian had come to San Benito because of an ongoing investigation into Tim's murder, that he had no interest in the politics of San Benito, perhaps he would let Brian go. And she wanted to tell him that even though she loved Brian, she valued him, Emilio, as a friend, and she respected what he was attempting to do for his country.

"What are you thinking about?" Brian asked.

"You." Juliana moved closer. "Always about you."

"Then I'm a lucky man." He put his arm around her and they leaned back against the wall. "Comfortable?"

"Mmm."

"Come closer." Brian pulled her across his knees and cradled her in his arms. "Is that better?"

"It's wonderful." Juliana smiled up at him. "Tell me about you."

"What do you want to know?"

"Everything. The kind of books you like to read, what kind of music you listen to. Who your first girl was...." Juliana paused. "Was she pretty?"

"All sixteen-year-old girls are pretty. Let me see... Her name was Marilee. I don't remember her last name. She had long blond hair that she wore in a braid down her back, blue eyes, and she was built like a truck driver with a bosom. A big bosom."

"Did you...?" Juliana looked up at him. "You know. Was she your first?"

"Yep." He kissed Juliana's nose. "Our romance lasted until I broke my arm playing football. Then she took up with the captain of the team."

"Wretched girl!" She punched him in the shoulder. "And wretched you."

"Who was your first love? Or would you rather not say?"

"I don't mind. His name was Jerome Simoski. He was blond and blue-eyed too. But he wasn't built like a truck driver, he was gorgeous!"

Brian clasped her firmly in his arms. "How long did this romance last?"

"Until I was six. Then we moved away."

"Until you were six!" Brian growled low in his throat and bit her ear. He liked talking to Julie this way. It was good to talk, to not think about what might happen tomorrow. Because he wanted to prolong the conversation, he said, "What's your idea of a perfect day?"

"You know what my idea of a perfect day is now." She grinned at him. "Before..." She wrinkled her forehead in concentration.... "Having a cup of hot chocolate in bed while I read the paper. Going to the beach. I love the sound of the waves and the smell of suntan oil, the feel of the sun melting right into my bones." She paused. "After the beach I liked to stop at a drive-in for a cheeseburger, then go home and get all spiffed up in my most elegant clothes and go to a concert. Mozart, not Ozzie Osborne."

"Onions on the cheeseburger?"

"Of course."

"You're my kind of woman. Will you marry me?"

"You betcha."

Brian kissed her. He held her close and thought how much he loved her. But he didn't speak of his love, nor did Juliana. They talked of inconsequential things, and dozed, and woke to talk again of where they would live when they were married. They picked out the names of the children they would have: Katie and

Elizabeth for the girls, Andrew and David for the boys. They kissed and clung and spoke of their love, but it was a night strangely without passion. There was a wonderful closeness between them, a closeness of the heart, rather than of the body.

Finally Juliana slept, but it was a long time before Brian did. His arms were around her, her head was on his shoulder. He loved her as he hadn't thought it ever possible to love. He wanted to have children with her, he wanted to grow old with her. But if he couldn't, then he wanted her to survive. He kissed the top of her head, thinking only of her.

Once the earth moved beneath them. She stirred and said, "What's that?"

"It's nothing," Brian lied. "Go back to sleep, love." He saw the bright orange flame through the windows and knew that the volcano was alive and breathing fire again.

Juan brought their breakfast of black beans, scrambled eggs and hard biscuits the next morning. He waited until they'd eaten, then, not looking at Brian said, "I'm going to take the Señorita Julie out for a while."

"Out? Out where?" Juliana asked.

"You'd like to see Rafael, wouldn't you?"

"Yes, of course I would. But..." She looked at Brian, then back to Juan. "No! No, I don't want to go. I want to stay here."

"Julie, please. Go with Juan. It'll be all right."

"No!" She felt fear building inside her. "I'm not going to leave you!"

"Then you may stay," Ricardo Zamora said from the doorway. "But you may not like what you see." He stepped into the room with Miguel Otero.

"Get her out of here, Zamora," Brian said.

"But if she wishes to stay, *señor...*"

Brian looked at Juan. "Get Julie out of here," he snapped.

"No! Brian, I won't go! I—" But Juan picked her up, and forcing her out the door said, "Come along, *muchacha.*"

The door slammed behind them.

"Put me down!" Juliana struggled and when Juan put her down she turned and looked back at the closed door, trembling with outrage and anger, and a terrible sickening fear. "Take me to Emilio!" she cried.

"I can't do that." Juan looked uncomfortable. "He doesn't want to see you."

"But I want to see him."

She started toward the cabin. Juan put his hand out to detain her. "Please, Señorita Julie, I have orders—"

The sound of a blow was heard. Then a laugh. A curse. Another blow.

Juliana's face paled. She clutched her stomach and doubled over as though the blows had been for her. Then she turned and ran toward the cabin.

Juan Garcia looked after her. He cursed long and hard in Spanish, but didn't attempt to stop her.

A rebel with a rifle blocked Juliana's way at the head of the stairs. She tried to knock him aside and when he put out his arm to push her back, Juan said, "Let her pass."

She ran past the guard and into the cabin just as Maria came into the room. "Julie!" Maria said. "Where are you going?"

"Where's Emilio?"

"In the office, but—"

Juliana ran past her. She flung open the office door, entered, and slammed it behind her.

Emilio half rose out of his chair. "What are you doing here?" His face was angry. "I left orders. I don't want to see you."

"But I want to see you!" Juliana ran across the room to the desk. "You've got to stop them," she cried.

"Stop who?"

"Your goons. Your strong men. They're in there now. They're beating Brian." She began to cry and that made her as furious with herself as she was with Emilio. "How can you do this?" she sobbed. "I liked you. I thought you were a decent human being."

Emilio looked at her. His face was as pale as hers now. He hesitated, then came around the desk to grasp her arms. "I loved you," he said. "You betrayed me."

"I didn't betray you." Juliana looked up at him. "Emilio, please, believe me. I never meant to hurt you." She hesitated, trying to find the words to tell him how she felt. "When you went away, when Tim was murdered, everybody said you were mixed up in his death. But I knew you weren't, Emilio. I knew you couldn't have killed Tim or anybody else." She clung to him. "Oh, please," she wept. "Don't let them kill Brian."

"They're only questioning him." Emilio looked away from her. "They won't kill him."

"They're only *questioning* him?" She clung to the desk for support. "Oh my God, Emilio, what's happened to you?"

He didn't answer. Instead he called out, "Maria! Maria, come in here." When the door opened and Maria came in, Emilio said, "Take Julie to your room and try to calm her down."

Maria looked at him, then at Juliana. She saw the tears and put her arms around Julie. "Come along," she said.

Juliana turned back to Emilio. "Please," she said, "If you ever loved me..."

"If I ever loved you..." For a moment his brown eyes softened with pain. Then he turned away from her and went to stand by the window.

He heard the door close behind the women. He looked out toward the room next to the stable, where Brian McNeely was being questioned.

When they were alone in Maria's room, Maria led Julie to the bed and sat beside her.

"What's happening?" Maria asked in a frightened voice. "I thought everything was all right again between you and Emilio. Then you ran away. *Por Dios*, Julie, everything happened at once. Old Manitura erupted and the camp was in an uproar, and you disappeared. I thought you were so afraid you ran into the jungle, then the next day Zamora said that you'd freed Señor McNeely and run away with him. Is that true?"

Juliana knuckled her tears away. "I freed him, Maria, but I didn't want to run away with him because of you and Rafael. I didn't want to leave you here."

"Oh, Julie." Maria hugged her. "This is all my fault." She got up and began to pace up and down the room. Finally she turned to Juliana and in a low voice said, "Zamora made me call. He couldn't know that you hadn't read the code book and he thought you knew too much."

"Knew too much? I didn't know anything!"

"But don't you see? They thought that because Tim was your brother he might have said something to you. He didn't like your dating Emilio and he might have..." She looked at Julie. "He might have said something to you about Emilio being involved with the revolution."

"Or about you being involved?" Juliana's expression darkened with anger. "Were you involved, Maria, even when Tim was alive?"

"No, of course not! How can you even ask such a thing?"

"Maybe because the minute he was dead you came back here."

"I didn't want to, but I had no choice!" There were tears in Maria's eyes. "My father ordered me back to San Benito and as soon as I arrived they brought me here to the mountains." She took a deep breath. "Emilio wasn't here. Zamora was in charge. He said if I didn't call you..." She bent her head and began to cry. "He threatened Rafael, Julie. He said if I didn't call you I'd never see Rafa again."

Juliana stared at Maria in horror, then she put her arms around her sister-in-law and said, "I'm sorry. Please don't cry, Maria. It's all right."

Maria shook her head. "No, it's not all right, Julie. I should have been stronger. I should have taken Rafael and tried to run away, as you did."

"But I didn't succeed, Maria." Juliana sat down on the bed and drew Maria down beside her. "But with Brian..." She hesitated. "If you could free Brian, the four of us could escape together."

"Rafa and I would slow you down." Maria shook her head. "Even you and Mr. McNeely didn't make it."

"Part of the reason we didn't was just plain bad luck, Maria. The other part..." Juliana summoned a smile. "We forgot for a while where we were. We became too involved with each other. We lingered when we should have been running."

"You're in love with him, aren't you?"

"Yes, Maria. We're going to be married as soon as we get back to Miami." Juliana took Maria's hands in hers. "We'll get back, Maria, all of us, if you'll help." Her face was tense with strain. "Miguel Otero and another man are with Brian now. They're trying to make him admit he's with the CIA. He isn't, Maria, but they'll beat him until he tells them something or he..." Juliana couldn't go on because her voice was choked with tears. "Please," she said. "Please, Maria, help us."

Maria looked at Juliana, then away. "I'm afraid," she whispered. "I want to help you, Julie, but I'm afraid of Miguel. If he caught me..." She covered her face with her hands.

Juliana didn't speak. She turned away from Maria and stared out of the window, stared out to where Miguel Otero and another man were questioning Brian.

Five minutes later Juan Garcia knocked on Maria's door. "I'm to take you back now, Señorita Julie," he said.

"Is Brian...?" She couldn't form the words.

"I stopped it. He's...he's not too badly off."

Juliana swallowed. She tried to keep her voice steady when she said, "Thank you, Juan."

"I couldn't have done it, as much as I wanted to, without Emilio's orders."

"Emilio's orders...?" For the first time since she and Brian had been captured, Juliana felt a small flare of hope. If Emilio had stopped the questioning, that meant he wasn't without compassion, that maybe he had believed her. Maybe he would help them. She looked down at Maria, who sat with bowed head, tears streaking her cheeks. For a moment Juliana rested her hand on Maria's head. "It's all right," she said. "Don't cry, Maria."

Brian lay on the straw mat, his face toward the wall, his hands tied behind his back. "It's not as bad as it looks," he said when Juliana ran to kneel beside him. "Juan came in before they killed me."

"Brian..." Juliana pressed her hand to her mouth.

"Take it easy, Julie. Just take it easy." One eye was swollen and there was a cut over the other. "It's okay." He tried to smile but his face hurt. "If you think I look bad, you should see the other two guys."

He struggled to a sitting position. "Get these ropes off me," he said.

"Yes, of course." She ran and knelt beside him. "I'm sorry," she whispered. She pulled on the ropes that bound him, tears of frustration running down her face when she couldn't untie them.

"Easy, love," Brian said. "That's it, you've got it now."

The ropes loosened. He massaged his wrists. Julie put her arms around him. "What have they done to you?" she whispered.

"Not as much as they wanted to. I got in a few licks. Damn near kicked Otero's kneecap off, and the other guy is going to walk bent over holding his groin for the next couple of hours." Brian flexed his shoulders. "Juan stopped them. I hope he doesn't get in trouble because of me."

"He won't. Emilio told him to stop it."

"Emilio? I'll be damned." Brian searched her face. "Are you all right?"

Juliana nodded. "Just scared, Brian." She touched the side of his face and tenderly kissed his bruised lips. Then she bathed his face and made him lie down on the straw mat. She sat beside him and held his hand when he closed his eyes to rest. She thought about Maria, who was too afraid to help them. And of Emilio. Emilio had stopped the beating. Did that mean he might help her and Brian? She leaned her back against the wall and closed her eyes. All they could do now was wait.

* * *

It was after midnight when they heard the whisper. "Julie? Julie, are you awake?"

Juliana closed her hand on Brian's arm. "Oh, God, Maria," she murmured as a flare of hope surged through her body. She stood up and moved cautiously to the door. "Maria?"

"I'm going to try to pry off the lock, Julie."

"Is it Maria?" Brian whispered. He put his arm around Juliana and leaned closer to the door. The sound of the scrape of metal was sharp in the quiet night. "Take it easy, Maria," he cautioned softly. "Don't try to hurry."

"The lock's too big." Maria's voice was frightened. "I don't think I can pry it off."

"Do you have a crowbar?" Brian forced himself to speak slowly.

"Yes, I . . . I think that's what it is."

"Okay. Put the narrow end under the hasp that's screwed onto the door. Now push the narrow end of the crowbar, where it's bent, between the wood and the metal."

"Into the part that's in the door?"

"Yes." Brian took a deep breath. "Between the part that's screwed in and the door."

"Yes, I see. What do I do now?"

"Push the crowbar downward toward the door."

"I can't. It won't move."

Brian felt Juliana's hand tighten on his arm. He put his hands on the door and leaned closer. "Did you bring a hammer, Maria?"

"No. Should I have? *Por Dios, señor*, I'll never be able to do this."

"Sure you will. Take it easy. See if you can find a rock."

"A rock. Wait . . . yes, I found one."

"Okay. Do you have a piece of cloth? A handkerchief?"

"I have a scarf."

"Wrap it around the rock, Maria. Now try to hammer the rock against the end of the crowbar."

"Wait. Yes, all right."

They heard the dull thud of rock hitting metal. Juliana tightened her grip on Brian's arm. Sweat trickled down her body. The door squeaked.

"That's it," Brian muttered. "Keep pushing, Maria, bear down."

"I'm . . . trying. I think I've got it. I—"

They heard her gasp. Then scream, "No! Let me go!"

Then the sound of a struggle, a slap, and Miguel Otero's voice snarling, "Get back to the house. I'm going to tell Zamora about this."

For a moment there was no sound except of Maria crying as she ran away. Then there was a knock on the door and Otero said, "So, you convinced your sister-in-law to help you, *gringa*. That was a mistake. You didn't do her any favor, you know. When Zamora hears about this he'll send the boy away. Then she'll do whatever we ask."

"No, please." Juliana pounded on the door with her fists. "It wasn't Maria's fault. I begged her to help us. She didn't want to, I made her do it."

"Perhaps you're more trouble that you're worth, *señorita gringa*. Or perhaps what you need is a man who can tame you. When we've finished off your friend you'll be my woman and I'll teach you how to behave properly." He chuckled. "Good night, *gringa*, sweet dreams."

Brian swore under his breath. He put his arms around Juliana and felt her trembling against him.

"What are we going to do?" she whispered. "Oh, Brian, what are we going to do?"

"We're not going to give up," he said. "We'll find a way, Julie." He drew her close again and held her tight. "We'll find a way," he said against her hair.

Chapter 17

They lay close together on the straw mat. Brian stroked her back and kissed the side of her face, meaning only to comfort her. But slowly, subtly, the warmth of comfort changed to the warmth of desire as the need to be even closer overwhelmed them. They undressed each other and Juliana opened her arms to receive him into her embrace.

Brian kissed her deeply, gently. His body was warm over hers, shielding and protecting her. Juliana lifted her body to his and there in the quiet of the night they made love. She closed her eyes as they began to move together. This time was different from the others because there was a need to express all that they felt in this moment, all that there might not be time to say later.

I give myself to you, Juliana said with the arms that held him.

As I give myself to you, Brian said with the mouth that sought hers.

They had never been so totally one with each other as they were that night, there on the straw mat with only the glimmer of the moon shining in from the small windows above them. In the final moment, when together they climbed the peak of their mutual passion, Brian said, "I love you, Julie. Now, forever."

"As I love you."

Hot tears streaked her face. He caught them on his lips and gave them back to her with a kiss. He soothed her with tender hands and whispered of his love. Then, not wanting to leave her, he rolled over so that her body rested on his, and together, their bodies still joined, they slept.

That afternoon the earth began to shake and the odor of sulfurous gas filled the air. The sky darkened, casting only the dimmest of lights into the place where they were held.

"It's the volcano." Juliana's voice was frightened. "Brian..." She tried to quell her rising panic. "Brian, we've got to get out of here."

"We will." He put his arms around her. "They've got to know the whole mountain is going to blow. They'll evacuate and take us with them."

At least they'd take Julie, Brian thought. Emilio won't let her die. The earth trembled beneath his feet. There was a roar like that of a train and the smell of sulphur grew stronger. He wanted to pound on the door, to scream for someone to let them out. Instead he took off his shirt, tore it in half, and when he had wet both halves he gave one to Juliana and said, "Cover your nose and mouth. It will help." He led her to the farthest corner of the room, and when they sat down, their backs against the wall, he drew her close.

The piece of his shirt was cool against her face, but Juliana took it away and said, "They'll take Maria and Rafael to safety. Emilio wouldn't risk their lives."

"Of course he wouldn't. Any more than he'd risk your life, Julie. If he thinks the danger is real, he'll get everybody out."

Almost everybody. Brian's arms tightened around her. "Maybe this isn't as bad as we think. Volcanoes have been known to get active like this, then simmer down without erupting. Maybe old Manitura's just letting off steam."

But Brian knew in his bones that the volcano was going to blow. He thought about Krakatoa, a volcano in Indonesia that had killed more than thirty-six thousand people. Of Mount Pelée in Martinique. For weeks Mount Pelée had rumbled ominous sounds of warning, a warning people chose to ignore. Then it blew, and in minutes thirty thousand people died in a rush of hot lava that set the city on fire and destroyed everyone and everything it its path.

That could happen here, it could happen anytime now. Emilio must know the danger the camp was in. Surely he was making preparations to leave. Any minute Juan Garcia would unlock the door and take Julie someplace where she'd be safe.

But it was late that afternoon before Juan unlocked the room where they were held. Another man stood guard with a rifle while Juan handed Brian a bag with two sandwiches and half a bottle of wine. "That's the best I could do," he said. "The camp's in an uproar."

"They're getting ready to leave?" A wave of relief flooded through Brian.

Juan shook his head. "What they're doing—Emilio and Zamora—is *arguing* about getting ready to leave." Juan's face showed his concern. "The others are afraid. They want to get out of here but Zamora says this is only a rumble. He says it'll calm down in a few days." Juan lowered his voice. "But the men are angry. They're turning away from Zamora and looking for Emilio to lead them out of here."

"He will," Julie said. "I know he will." She looked at Juan. "What about Maria and Rafael? Last night..." Juliana hesitated, wondering if Juan knew that last night Maria had tried to help them escape.

"Maria and the boy are locked in her room," Juan said. "On orders from Zamora."

"Is she..." Juliana clenched her hands into fists. "Is she all right?"

Juan nodded, looking embarrassed. "Nobody's hurt her, *señorita*. She's related to half the camp. But Emilio and Zamora had a hell of a fight about her trying to help you."

"It's turning into a power struggle between Zamora and Emilio, isn't it?" Brian said.

Juan nodded. "Zamora wants to overthrow the government so that he can be the next president. Sanchez-Fuentes is a no-good son of a crocodile who needs to be hung from the rafters of the *palacio* by his..." Juan looked at Julie and cleared his throat. "By his thumbs," he finished. "But sometimes I wonder if Zamora would be any better. San Benito's suffered too long and we have struggled too hard to wind up with another dictator. Emilio wouldn't be like that. He's a true patriot. He loves San Benito, but with a love that's without political ambition." Juan ran a hand across his bearded face. "I can't believe he'd stand by and let Zamora take over. Emilio would make a good president; the people would follow him if he had the courage to stand up to Zamora."

Juan's eyes met Brian's. With a worried sigh he said, "We can't delay much longer here in the mountains, *señor*. We're too close to Manitura. When it blows—" Suddenly the earth shook again and a terrible roaring sounded. The guard at the door swore and said, "We're all going to die if somebody doesn't give the order to leave. What in the hell is the matter with Zamora? Does he think he's God, that he can defy Manitura? It's raining ash, the trees are covered, birds are dying. What in the hell is he waiting for?"

"Calm down, *compadre*," Juan said. "The order will come soon."

"And if it doesn't?" Brian moved closer to Juan. "You've got to let Julie go," he said quietly.

Juan shifted uncomfortably and started toward the door. "You're a decent man, Juan. I can't believe you'd let her die, locked up like this, unable to escape the volcano."

"Please, *señor*..." Juan edged toward the door. The guard looked at him, frowned and said, "Come on. I want to find out what in the hell they're doing about getting us out of here."

Juan glanced at Brian. "I'll do what I can when the time comes," he whispered.

The day passed. Juan didn't return. The volcano rumbled, making the earth tremble and lighting the sky with a demonic glare. The air in their small prison smelled of sulfur and smoke. Time and again they wet the remnants of Brian's shirt. As frightened as she'd ever been in her life, for herself and Brian, for Rafael and Maria, Juliana tried not to speak of her fear. "Juan will come back," she said again and again, as if the repetition soothed her. "If there's a real emergency, if the volcano really blows, he'll let us out."

"Of course he will," Brian said. But if Juan waited until the volcano exploded there wouldn't be time for any of them to get out. When Mount Pelée blew, the fire of lava raced down the slopes at more than a hundred miles an hour. No one escaped.

But we'll escape, Brian told himself. I won't let Julie die this way. Frantically he looked around for something, anything that might aid in their escape. He found a pointed rock and began to scrape the dirt floor near the back wall. If the foot-thick wood didn't go too far down maybe he could dig under it. Juliana found another rock. She knelt beside him and began to dig. Two hours later Brian said, "It's no use, Julie. The planks are sunk too far into the ground."

Darkness fell. Brian and Juliana sat together on the straw mat. He kept talking. He told her about growing up in San Francisco, about his hitch in the navy, the four years at UCLA and a year of prelaw before he had been picked up by the agency.

"I met Tim in Texas," Brian said. "It was my first job. Tim had been in for five or six years by then and he showed me the ropes. We became friends and once in a while he'd tell me about his little sister." Brian couldn't see Juliana's face, but he put his arm around her and pulled her closer. "He told me what a holy terror you were." He grinned at her. "I should have listened to him."

"Beast! Just for that I'm going to..." But the roar of the volcano drowned her voice. "Oh God," she said as she clung to Brian. "I'm so afraid." She buried her face against his throat. "We're not going to get out of here." She wept. "We've had all we're ever going to have. We—"

"Wait." Brian grasped her firmly by the arms. "I think I heard something."

Juliana held her breath. Then she heard it, the scrape of metal against the lock. Brian pulled her to her feet.

The door opened. Emilio said, "Julie?"

"Yes! Oh thank God! Emilio—"

"There's no time to talk." He thrust Maria, who was holding Rafael, into the room. "I want you to get them out of here, McNeely," Emilio said. "There's a jeep at the end of the trail to your right. Here's the key."

"You'd better come with us, Martinez," Brian said. "The volcano's going to blow anytime now."

"I can't leave until the men do. We'll be out of here by morning."

Juliana put her hand on Emilio's arm, all that had happened in the past forgotten now because Emilio had come. He was, after all, the kind of man she'd known he was. "Please come with us," she said.

Before he could answer, Rafael, who'd been wrapped up in a blanket, poked his head out and said, "I can't breathe. Why does everything smell so funny? Why is the sky on fire?"

"Shh, Rafa." Maria kissed his cheek. "We're going soon, then it will be better."

"Is *Tía* Julie coming too?"

"Yes, Rafa." Maria's voice was a nervous whisper. "Let's get out of here," she begged.

"Yes, go now, before Zamora discovers what I've done." Emilio handed Brian a gun. "Take this," he said. "Use it if you have to." He looked at Juliana, then away. "Keep her safe," he said.

"Emilio..." Tears welled in her eyes. "Emilio, I don't know what to say." She kissed his cheek. "Thank you," she whispered. "God bless."

Emilio looked at her for a moment. Then, without a word, he turned and disappeared into the darkness.

"Come on," Brian said. "Stay close behind me, bend low. Don't speak unless it's absolutely necessary."

They crept out the door toward the jungle trail to their right. If they could make it that far... Suddenly a figure loomed ahead of them in the darkness.

"Halt!" Miguel Otero said. "What the hell—?"

Brian hit him with the butt of the gun Emilio had given him. Otero staggered back. He tried to draw the pistol from his belt but he was too late. Brian hit him again and he fell without a sound.

"Come on!" Brian whispered. "Keep down."

They slipped into the jungle. Behind them they could hear the murmur of voices. Above them Manitura belched flame and smoke. Rafael began to whimper in fright and struggled to be put down. "Give me the boy," Brian said. He turned back the blanket that covered Rafael's face. "Let's leave this off so you can see what's going on," he said to Rafael. "I'm going to put you on my back and I want you to hang on. You be the guide and tell me if there's anything up ahead. Okay?"

"Okay!" Without another word Rafael put his arms around Brian's neck and wrapped his legs around Brian's waist.

They plunged through the jungle. When they saw the jeep, Brian stopped. "Do you know the way out of here?" he asked Maria. She nodded and he said, "Sit up front with me. Julie, you and Rafael get in the back." He got in and started the jeep, put it into reverse, then wheeled it around and started down the path that led to the main road.

"I want to go down to the beach," he told Maria. "I'm going to try to get us on a boat."

Juliana pulled Rafael onto her lap and put her arms around him. "Don't you think we'd be safer in the city?"

"Not from the lava flow. We'd be better off heading out to sea." The jeep jolted over a rock and Brian

cursed. Speed was important but they couldn't afford
the jeep breaking down. He forced himself to drive
slowly until they reached the main road. "Which way
to the beach?" he asked Maria.

She pointed ahead. "There'll be a gravel road on
your left about a mile farther on. It leads down the
mountain to the beach."

The jeep sped on for a mile, then slowed as Brian
searched for the gravel road. The rumbles from the
volcano grew louder. By the light of the orange flames
that spewed from the crater's mouth they saw trees
uprooted. Boulders thundered down the mountain. A
black cloud filled with lightning obliterated the moon.

Rafael clung to Juliana as the jeep jolted over the
rough road. "How much farther?" she asked Maria.

"Twenty minutes." Maria's voice was frightened.

The night had been made in hell. Above the rumble
and roar of the volcano they heard the frantic chatter
of monkeys in the trees on either side of the road and
the cry of birds. Small animals, desperate to escape,
darted out in front of the jeep. Hot ash pelted down
on them. Rafael sobbed; Juliana tried to shield him
with her body.

Brian gripped the steering wheel tightly. He narrowed his eyes, trying to see through the falling ash
and the cloud of smoke that was slowly covering the
island. "Hang on," he shouted as he pressed his foot
down on the gas pedal. Any second now the whole
damn mountain was going to blow!

He wished that Julie were beside him instead of
Maria, but he needed Maria to guide him down to the
beach. Please, God, he silently prayed, let there be a

boat when we reach the water. His eyes stung from the smoke. He slapped a smoldering cinder off his arm. "Get down on the floor," he yelled to the two women.

Maria didn't move. "Get down!" Brian roared.

"No. There's a curve just ahead. Beyond there's a small road leading off to the right. That's the one we have to take. It follows the mountain and drops down to the sea."

"Okay. Thanks. Get down." Brian pushed Maria to the floor. He maneuvered the curve and saw the road to the right. It led around the side of the mountain. He turned onto it and reduced his speed. The headlight beams cut through the darkness and Brian swore. The road was no more than twelve feet wide. There was a sheer drop on one side; he'd have to hug the side of the mountain. He—

Suddenly, just ahead, there was a terrible crashing roar. Brian hit the brakes just as a cascade of rocks came thundering down. He threw himself down on the seat, trying to cover Maria's body with his own.

The crashing of boulders threw up dust and chips of rock. It went on and on and when it stopped, Brian sat up listening to the falling clatter of stones below. He pulled Maria up off the floor, then leaned back to help Juliana and Rafael. "Are you all right?" he asked.

"Yes, yes, I think so." She had her arms around Rafael. "Is Maria all right?"

"Yes, I'm..." Maria stared at the landslide. "Oh, my God!" she cried. "The road's blocked."

Brian stared at the path ahead. Rocks were piled high. There was no way around them, at least not with

the jeep. "How much farther to the beach?" he asked
Maria.

"Two or three miles," she said. "it's not far, but the
jeep—"

"Forget the jeep, we'll walk." He got out, gave
Maria a hand, then took Rafael from Juliana and
helped her down. He put an arm around her. "It's
going to be okay, Julie," he said. "We're going to
make it."

Juliana looked at the pile of rocks blocking their
way. "I guess we're going to have to climb over the
rocks," she said with an exaggerated groan.

"I guess we are." Brian put Rafael on his back,
said, "Hang on, boy," and started out.

Maria looked at Julie. "We don't have any choice,
do we?" she said.

"Nope." Juliana took her sister-in-law's hand.
"Maybe it's not as bad as it looks."

But it was. It was the most difficult thing Juliana
had ever done in her life, even harder than the climb
she'd made with Brian the night she helped him escape. Brian, burdened with Rafael, helped the two
women as much as he could. But there was no time for
coaxing, no time to be considerate. He had to get them
off this side of the mountain before there was another
rock slide. They had to reach the beach before the
volcano blew.

Twenty minutes later, battered and bruised, they
were on the other side of the slide.

"Can't we rest for a few minutes?" Maria asked.

"No, sorry." Brian looked up at the volcano. "Let's
move it." He turned away and began to walk. When

the track went downhill he jogged and made them jog. "Keep up! Move it!" he barked at Julie and Maria. He knew he sounded like a marine drill instructor, but he had to get them to the beach. Once Maria stumbled and fell, and Julie said, "She's got to rest."

"She can rest when we get to the beach." Brian helped Maria to stand. "We're almost there," he told her. "You can make it."

"Yes..." Maria gasped for air. "Yes, I can make it."

They ran on. The earth quivered beneath their feet. Rocks tumbled and fell in front of them. Brian took Rafael off his back and wrapped his arms around him. Rafael didn't speak, but his dark eyes were wide with fright.

Juliana's legs hurt. Her side burned with pain and her chest heaved with the effort to breathe. She wanted to beg Brian to stop, but she didn't. She staggered, slipped, and fell to her knees, but got up before Brian could see that she'd fallen.

The road evened out. Ahead they saw palm trees. Beyond lay the sea.

"We made it," Brian told Rafael. "We made it, boy." He stopped and looked back at the two women. By the light from the terrible orange glow in the sky he saw the exhaustion on their faces. "Only a little farther," he told them. "You can rest while I find a boat."

They struggled forward. When they reached the sand Brian said, "Rest here, I'll be right back." He put Rafael down. "You take care of your mother and Julie until I get back," he told the boy.

Some of the fear went out of Rafael's face. "Okay," he said. "But don't be gone too long."

"I won't." Brian ruffled the boy's hair. Then he bent down to where Julie lay prone on the sand and quickly kissed her. "If it blows before I come back," he said in a low voice, "take Maria and the boy and head for the water. Swim out as far as you can."

"Brian?" She threw her arms around his neck, hiding her face against his shoulder for a moment. Then she released him.

He ran down the deserted beach trying to find anything that would float. Ahead of him he saw a dock protruding into the water. Near the end of it a boat was moored. He ran out onto the dock. It was a rowboat and he thanked God the oars were in place.

Brian whirled around and ran, calling out, "Julie! I've found a boat. Come on! Hurry!"

They ran up the beach toward him. He scooped Rafael up in his arms and took Julie's hand just as a thunderous detonation shook the ground beneath their feet.

"Quick!" Brian ran out onto the dock. Maria clambered into the boat and reached up for Rafael. He handed the boy down, then helped Julie. When he was in the boat he freed the mooring rope and picked up the oars. As he bent his back to the task he looked up at Manitura. Two fiery craters glowed like blast furnaces near the summit. At that moment the moon, full and fat and yellow, came out from behind a cloud. Then the orange flames shot up and the moon was obliterated.

"My God!" Maria drew Rafael closer. "Oh, my God!"

But Juliana was too frightened to speak. She looked at Brian. His face, bronzed by the flames in the sky, was determined and unafraid. His eyes met hers, and from somewhere deep inside her Julie found the strength to say, "We're going to make it, Brian. We're going to make—"

The explosion ripped the words from her mouth. Two huge black clouds of volcanic material shot out of the mountain, straight up, expanding across the sky, turning the moon to fire.

Explosion followed explosion in throbbing, pulsating roars.

"Look!" Maria screamed, her expression strained as she pointed to a bright line of flame that raced down the slopes to the land below, setting fire to everything it touched, a boiling red river that seemed to flow straight from hell.

Brian stared upward, then with a curse bent his back to the oars. He heard Maria weeping for the people who'd been left behind, for Juan and Emilio and all the others who might not have made it out. He looked at Julie, frozen and still in front of him, her eyes wide with horror. He wanted to tell her everything that was in his heart, but there was no time for the telling now. Maybe later, when this terrible night ended. If it ever ended.

The mail boat from Belém picked them up two hours later. There were other survivors aboard, huddled together on the narrow deck, watching the burning flow of lava and the hundreds of fires it had caused sear their land to ashes.

When the hour grew late the other passengers went below. One of the crew found a deck chair for Maria and Rafael, and after Juliana had covered them with a blanket she went to stand at the rail with Brian.

"All those people," she said, as she looked back at San Benito. "Juan, Emilio..." She couldn't go on.

"They could have got out." Brian put his arms around her. "San Benito will have to be rebuilt," he said. "If Emilio is alive, he'll be the man to rebuild it."

"Yes, if he's alive." Juliana looked up at him. Her face was dirty, her hair disheveled. Her shirt was torn and her knees were skinned. But he thought she'd never looked more beautiful. And suddenly Brian knew that Juliana would always be beautiful to him because he loved her, because he would always love her.

They kissed, there in the glow of moon fire. The shadow of a smile touched her lips, her eyes drifted shut. "Don't ever leave me," she whispered as his arms tightened around her.

"I never will," he said. And knew that he never would.

Epilogue

The church was quiet. Spring flowers bedecked the altar. Sun streamed in the stained-glass windows making patterns of light on the red carpet, shining down on the small group gathered before the priest.

"In the name of the Father, and of the Son, and of the Holy Ghost," the priest said as he looked down at the child asleep in her father's arms. He picked the baby up and handed her to her godfather. "I baptize you..."

Katie Anne McNeely opened her eyes. The corners of her mouth turned down, and she let out a howl that soared to the rafters of the church.

Jack Kelly gingerly held the small bundle of fury while her face turned as red as her hair.

The priest sprinkled water on her head. "Katie Anne..." The rest of the words were lost in her indignant screams.

"I'm sorry, Father," Juliana murmured.

"Not at all, my dear." The priest wiped the small head, took the baby from Jack Kelly, and handed her back to her father.

Brian put his face against his daughter's and said, "That's enough, Miss Katie. That's enough, my small love."

She hiccuped, wrapped her finger around his thumb, and smiled up at him.

"Your daughter seems to have a will of her own," the priest murmured.

"Just like her mother," Brian said with a sigh. He looked at Juliana, still just a little angry because last night Lieutenant Dan Perry had phoned and said, "Come and get your wife, McNeely."

"What is it this time?" Brian had growled.

"A Save the Porpoise demonstration. She and about fifty of her friends staged a sit-in this morning. Wouldn't let the commercial fishermen get to their boats. Said they were catching porpoises in their nets."

Brian had lectured her all the way home. "Tomorrow's the christening," he'd scolded. "How could you leave Katie that way?"

"Maria loves taking care of the baby. So does Rafa. Everything's set for tomorrow. The caterer will have the buffet ready by the time we get back from the church."

When they went into the house she kissed Katie Anne on both cheeks and was rewarded with a beatific smile. "Dinnertime," she said.

"What did you do about feeding her today?"

"I had enough bottles ready just in case—"

"Just in case you were locked up for a few days? Damn it all, Julie—"

"Shh," Juliana said. "You'll upset her." She carried Katie over to the sofa and sat down with her. Then she opened her blouse, and cradling the baby close, began to feed her. "Isn't she an angel?" she whispered as she kissed the small fingers. "Isn't she the most perfect baby you've ever seen?"

The glow from the lamp touched the faces of mother and child, and as suddenly as it had come, Brian's anger faded. He looked down at the two people he loved most in the world and a lump the size of a basketball formed in his throat, the same lump that formed every time he watched Juliana with the baby.

Now he looked at his wife across the baptismal font. Marriage to Juliana had been everything he thought it would be—and more. There were times like yesterday when his heart filled with a love that went beyond words.

Juliana looked up and saw Brian watching her. Her cinnamon eyes widened. Her lips parted and he saw the catch of breath in her throat. For that brief moment they were alone in the church. Then Rafael tugged at her sleeve and the spell was broken.

Katie Anne was asleep by the time they returned to the house they'd moved into six months before her birth. Juliana took her upstairs to the room adjoining their bedroom and put her in her crib. Then she went downstairs to join their guests.

She came into the room just as Jack said, "I had some good news today, Brian."

Brian handed Juliana a glass of champagne. "Let's hear it."

"It came in on the wire last night." Jack turned to Maria. "I want you to hear this too," he said. "It's about San Benito."

"San Benito? What is it?"

"The revolution's over, Maria. Sanchez-Fuentes is in Brazil; Emilio Martinez is the new president."

Maria stared up at him. "Thank God," she said.

Brian raised his glass of champagne. "Let's drink to San Benito," he said. "To Emilio, and to good men like Juan Garcia."

Juliana raised her glass. "To Emilio," she said.

Most of the guests left in the afternoon; only Maria, Rafael, and Jack Kelly stayed on until evening. When Rafael fell asleep, Jack carried him up and put him to bed in Katie Anne's room. When he came back he sat next to Maria on the sofa and unself-consciously reached for her hand.

Juliana raised her eyebrows, but didn't say anything.

"They've started going out," Brian said later when he and Juliana were alone. "Do you mind?"

Juliana shook her head. "I did at first, but not now. Maria's young, she has her whole life ahead of her. And Jack's a great guy. I hope everything turns out well for them."

"So do I." Brian turned the lights off, and together they went upstairs to their room. When they were inside Brian took Julie in his arms and kissed her. "Wear the white gown tonight," he said against her lips.

The white nightgown she'd bought in Tenango a year ago. Juliana leaned her head against Brian's shoulder, filled with love and remembrance. When she stepped away from him she took the gown out of the drawer, undressed, and slipped it on.

Brian took her hand and together they went into the baby's room. By the dim light of the bedside lamp they looked down at their daughter. She lay on her stomach, small hands curled into fists, her mouth curved in a smile.

Brian laid a finger against one rosy cheek. "Look what our love has made," he said. He put his arm around Juliana and together they watched their baby daughter sleep.

* * * * *

Starting in October...

SHADOWS ON THE NILE

by

Heather Graham Pozzessere

A romantic short story in six installments from best-selling author Heather Graham Pozzessere.

The first chapter of this intriguing romance will appear in all Silhouette titles published in October. The remaining five chapters will appear, one per month, in Silhouette Intimate Moments' titles for November through March '88.

Don't miss "*Shadows on the Nile*"—a special treat, coming to you in October. Only from Silhouette Books.

Be There!

IMSS-1